Gillian was holding her waist and pulling her closer. Their kiss deepened. Colleen thrust her fingers into Gillian's thick hair. She breathed in the scent of Gillian's cologne, felt the hard, muscled body mold into her own. Gillian clung to Colleen's waist, possessive and demanding. She roughly pulled the silk shirt from Colleen's pants and stopped their kiss only long enough to unbutton the shirt and unzip the pants. Her mouth possessed Colleen's again as she stripped Colleen naked and pushed her onto the couch.

Gillian was dressed only in a long, white T-shirt and white bikini underwear. It was her favorite lounging attire, and Colleen loved to see her in it. Now Colleen pulled the T-shirt off as they fell against the couch. She ran her hands over the sculpted body and cupped the full breasts. She moaned involuntarily as Gillian kissed her neck and bit her tenderly on the shoulder. Gillian's hands were all over her, her touch alternately soft and hard. Her whispered promises of what she was going to do sent shivers up Colleen's spine.

About the Author

Barbara Johnson is the author of the phenomenally successful *The Beach Affair,* which stayed on the Lambda Rising Bookstore's top-ten best-selling list for almost a year. She's also the author of *Stonehurst,* and has short stories in five Naiad anthologies: *The Mysterious Naiad, The First Time Ever, Dancing in the Dark, Lady Be Good,* and the upcoming *Touch of Your Hand.*

Bad Moon RISING

BARBARA JOHNSON

THE NAIAD PRESS, INC.
1998

Printed in the United States of America on acid-free paper
First Edition

Editor: Christine Cassidy
Cover designer: Bonnie Liss (Phoenix Graphics)
Typesetter: Sandi Stancil

Library of Congress Cataloging-in-Publication Data

Johnson, Barbara, 1955–
   Bad moon rising / by Barbara Johnson.
      p.   cm.
   ISBN 1-56280-211-9 (alk. paper)
   1. Lesbians – Fiction   I. Title.
PS3560.037174B425 1998
813'.54—dc21

98-13231
CIP

For Daddy
1923-1993

Acknowledgments

A GREAT BIG thanks to all the readers who bought *The Beach Affair* and made it such a great success.

And to some special people — Christine Cassidy for helping make Colleen grow; Kathleen DeBold for loving me still after all these years; Katherine V. Forrest for her encouragement and advice; Vanessa Lowe for being Naiad's number one fan; and Sandy Marks for her pep talks and unfailing belief in me — I say thank you from the bottom of my heart. To Jane Troxell and Kathy Weems, thank you for creating safe places for women and the opportunities for authors like myself to share our work. Also, to Deacon McCubbin and Jim Bennett at Lambda Rising, thank you for your wonderful support to a "local girl." You've been a part of my life for 23 years.

Thanks also to the following bookstores for helping the success of *The Beach Affair* by hosting signings: HerStory Bookstore (Hellam, PA), Lambda Rising (D.C. and Rehoboth Beach, DE), Lammas Women's Books and More (Baltimore and D.C.), Out & About Books (Orlando, FL), Phoenix Rising (Richmond, VA), and Purple Moon (Fredericksburg, VA). These gay and lesbian bookstores are important to our community. Please support them.

Prologue

In the Southeast district of Washington, D.C., Amber Rose bolted from the old warehouse that served as a makeshift film studio. The driving rain felt needle-sharp against her skin as she dodged potholes and oil slicks in the crumbling pavement. She tripped on a broken chunk of asphalt near her trailer, and then made her way unsteadily up the shallow wooden steps. The warped door was stuck again. She pushed hard and fell painfully to one knee as the door snapped open. The combined smells of stale cigarette smoke, spilled booze, mildew, and cheap perfume rushed at her and made her gag.

Amber crawled the rest of the way into the trailer. She just didn't have the energy to stand. The shoot was taking much too long. Jackson had yelled at her again, telling her to go to her trailer and do whatever it took to get her act together. She knew what she needed. The problem was, her supplier hadn't been getting her any good stuff lately. How did Hobie expect her to function on such low-grade heroin? She sat on the floor and looked around. Just where had she hidden it this time? She gazed intently at the shredded edge of the couch and allowed her mind to go blank.

When she finally stood, Amber didn't know how long she'd been sitting on the floor. All she knew now was that she was soaked through, her bones ached, and her right knee throbbed with pain. She looked at her knee and was surprised to see it scraped and bloody. The thin robe she'd put on over her sheer pink negligee hadn't afforded any protection against the rain or the threadbare carpet.

In the tiny kitchen, she put the kettle on for tea and wiped the blood from her knee. She slipped an old Melissa Etheridge tape into the boom box. "Come to my window," Melissa sang. The throaty plea made Amber smile. A quick trip to the bedroom to strip off the negligee and replace it with old jeans and an oversize sweatshirt made her feel human again. She winced as she noticed the track marks showing faintly through the heavy makeup on her arms. They only made her more determined, however, to find her hidden stash. When she concealed it so well, sometimes she didn't know if she was trying to protect the heroin or herself.

Amber began pulling clothes out of the drawers. Nothing there. She opened several jars of makeup and cold cream. Again, nothing. The mirror above the built-in dresser caught her eye. Who was that looking at her? She moved closer and stared at her reflection. The girl who looked out at her was once considered beautiful. Girl? Hell, she was an old woman at 30.

Her blue eyes were pale to the point of being almost colorless. The heavy black mascara and eyeliner only emphasized dark circles and wrinkles that were not laugh lines. Full lips, stained blood red, shrieked for attention. Blonde hair, once lush and full, fell limply to her shoulders. The makeup girl had tried her best with gel and hairspray, but the hot lights didn't take long to undo her work — not to mention Amber's mad dash through the rain. At least Jackson didn't insist on platinum blonde anymore. The dyes had burned her scalp.

Amber dragged the sweatshirt off. She was thin to the point of emaciation, but knew that didn't seem to matter in this business. In fact, lots of guys really dug the skinny zonked-out look known in the modeling world as "heroin chic." A recent video review in *Hustler* had even christened her the "Kate Moss fuck-alike." It was meant to be a compliment.

If anyone cared enough to ask, she told them she was anorexic. But it was the drugs that kept her weight off. She turned sideways. She still had nice breasts. Perky. She was glad she'd resisted the pressure to get bigger implants. Just big enough to look good on film. Jackson liked the fact that her

3

nipples were always hard. He enjoyed rubbing rouge on them, and would squeeze them painfully. Amber grimaced at the memory.

She pulled the sweatshirt back on and abandoned the woman in the mirror. If she dwelled on her situation for too long, she would disgust herself, and then the thoughts of suicide would creep in. It would be so easy. Just a little more than usual. A sweet euphoria would overcome her and she would sleep forever. She blinked to shake the ideas out of her mind and began her search once more. Nothing in the bathroom or the tiny closet. The big vase on the floor turned up empty too.

The kettle started whistling, setting her nerves more on edge. Her earlier fix was really wearing off and she became more frantic in her search. Trembling hands tore the sheets off the bed and overturned the mattress, scattering ancient dust bunnies into the damp, stagnant air. The noise from the kitchen seemed to get louder, the whistle a shrill scream. Ready to scream herself, Amber went into the kitchen and switched off the stove. Her hands shook more violently as she poured the scalding water into a mug over a used Earl Grey teabag.

Melissa continued singing. "Come feed your hunger, your thirst." Amber couldn't help but smile at the irony. Heroin and tea. That would satisfy both. Now, if she could only find the heroin ... She took a quick gulp of tea. Too hot, it burned her tongue and scalded her throat. She began to cough. Shit! Jackson would kill her if she fucked up the blow job scene this afternoon.

A flash of white caught her eye. There, over by the boom box. She abandoned the tea and crowed with delight as she discovered the cellophane packet of white powder. Funny how these things worked out, she thought as she dug a needle and rubber tourniquet out of her battered purse. She'd torn the place apart, and the damn stuff had been sitting on the table the whole time. In plain view too. She was getting careless.

In the minuscule bathroom, she worked automatically to heat the heroin, find a vein, and shoot up. The drug hit quickly. It always felt at first as if someone slugged the side of her head, but then her jitters dissolved as the familiar euphoria set in. The fire burned through her veins, faster than usual. She took a deep breath and walked slowly and unsteadily out to the living room. She noticed that the Melissa tape had quit. Ever more dizzy, she stumbled as she approached the table. Her legs felt heavy. Maybe the tea would help. Blurry-eyed, she reached for it, but her fingers couldn't quite grasp the mug. It crashed to the floor and shattered as she slumped over.

Chapter One

Insurance investigator Colleen Fitzgerald snapped shut her compact as she heard footsteps approaching her office. She'd been admiring the sleekness of her new haircut, wondering how Gillian would like it. Now that she thought about it, she wondered when Gillian would even see it. It had been almost three weeks since they'd been together, despite Gillian's assurances that she'd come to Washington soon. Still, Colleen decided that if *she* lived at the beach, she wouldn't want to move to the city either.

The footsteps paused outside her closed door, then continued down the hall. Colleen felt both relief and disappointment. It was almost quitting time, and she didn't want to get stuck in a meeting. Then again, it had been such a long time since her last assignment — three months, in fact, since she'd gotten back from Rehoboth Beach and her first solo investigation. Tired of checking statistics and reviewing write-ups for other investigators, she wondered briefly if staying with the investigative firm of Sampson and Rhoades, Inc. had been a smart career move.

Colleen sighed. She had only herself to blame. During her investigation into the death of bodybuilder Candy Emerson, Colleen had unwittingly discovered that Kevin Sampson — the man who'd assigned her the case and one of the company's owners — had been taking bribes to hurry along certain investigations. As full partner, he couldn't just be fired; there were delicate negotiations and damage-control publicity to perform. The other partner, Cranford Rhoades, hadn't wanted Colleen involved on a new case, and possibly out of town, until things had been completely settled.

Colleen looked at her watch. Four-thirty. Half an hour to go. As she debated whether or not to call Gillian, the phone rang.

"Fitzgerald here," she answered, her heart beating in anticipation.

"You sound so sexy when you're breathless," a male voice responded.

She tried to keep the disappointment out of her voice. "Oh, hi, Brian."

"Tut-tut. No need to sound so enthusiastic. I assume you haven't heard from the oh-hallowed one?"

"I'm sure she'll call tonight. She's very busy." Colleen could visualize Brian rolling his eyes.

"Hmmm. Yes, I suppose teaching one aerobics class a day would really wear one out. And let's not forget all that lying around in the sun. Poor, exhausted Gillian!"

"It's October, Brian. She's not lying around in the sun."

"Oh, I forgot. Lying around in a tanning booth, then."

"Be nice to me, Brian."

"Of course I'll be nice to you," he cooed. "That's why I'm calling. I want you to come to dinner tonight. I have someone for you to meet."

"Male or female?"

He clicked his tongue. "Do you think I'd try to set you up with someone while you're busy pining over that butch little beach bunny?"

"That's exactly what I think."

"How right you are. And I won't take no for an answer."

Colleen thought about the prospect of another long evening alone. "Well, I suppose dinner wouldn't hurt. Where and when?"

"Food for Thought at six. Wear something sexy."

The phone clicked in her ear. Colleen tried to stay annoyed with Brian, but she knew he was only looking out for her. She couldn't understand why Gillian seemed so reluctant to come live with her. Or at least nearby. Their romance had ignited so quickly in the scorching summer atmosphere of the Delaware resort town. Perhaps too quickly? She opened her desk drawer and looked at the picture of Gillian she kept hidden under her papers.

The brown-haired woman smiled out at her, a mischievous gleam sparkling from dark green eyes. Tight blue bicycle shorts and a sleeveless white T-shirt showed off a tanned, muscular body. Colleen looked at the full lips and imagined them kissing her. She could feel the familiar exhilaration begin as she remembered the big, strong hands exploring her body. Frustrated in more ways than one, Colleen slammed her drawer and shut away the vision. She and Gillian needed to have a talk, and soon!

Colleen packed up her briefcase. She had more boring reports to go over, which she used to help her sleep. Maybe dinner tonight would evolve into a movie too. Then she wouldn't need the reports. She ran her hand self-consciously over her new shorter hair and left the office.

The October day was cool enough for the light wool blazer she wore, but the bitter cold of winter was a long way off. She loved this time of year best — the changing leaves, the cool temperatures, the anticipation of holidays to come. She couldn't help but smile as she made her way to the crowded subway. With yams and whipcream-slathered pumpkin pie in her thoughts, she didn't even mind when a rambunctious trio of kids bumped her out of the way as they raced for a seat.

She got off the subway at DuPont Circle and took the Q Street exit. It was only a short walk to her apartment building. She stopped briefly in the foyer for her mail, then guiltily pushed the elevator button. When she first returned from her case in Rehoboth, she'd vowed to use the stairs instead. Gillian's fitness-conscious influence had even induced her to sign up for aerobics classes, but they just weren't the same without Gillian to teach them. After the initial six-week period, Colleen hadn't signed up again. She much preferred the private workouts that Gillian gave her whenever they got together. But those were getting less and less frequent. Gillian had come to Washington only once in the three months or so since they'd been dating, and was often "unavailable" when Colleen wanted to come visit on the weekend.

The apartment was unusually quiet as she opened the door. No incessant meowing greeted her. Then she saw the tangled mess of phone and answering machine on the floor. "Okay, you bad kitty, where are you hiding?" At least the cat hadn't disconnected anything this time. She counted three red blinks on the answering machine.

"C'mon out, Smokey, all is forgiven," she crooned as she plopped on the couch that also served as her bed. She set the answering machine on the table and hit the play button.

Beep. "This is Dr. Crenshaw's office calling to remind you of your dental appointment this Friday."

Colleen made a face. As if going to the dentist wasn't bad enough, they had to call and remind you of it. She opened her mail.

Beep. "Colleen. It's your mother. Don't forget you're coming over for dinner Saturday night. And guess what . . . William's coming too! Give me a call when you get home."

Oh great, she thought, what a way to follow a visit to the dentist. Dinner with the he-who-can-do-no-wrong brother. She had to find some way to get out of it. She tossed aside the phone bill. It was too high, as usual.

Beep. "Hey, sweetie. Tried to call you at the

10

office, but you left early. I know it's been a while since we've seen each other, but I wanted you to know I'm thinking of you. Sea Witch Weekend will be here in three weeks, and I thought you could come up for the revelry. Let me know. Bye."

The low, sexy voice never failed to cause a reaction. Colleen felt her cheeks grow hot just thinking about Gillian. Wasn't it just typical that the one day she left early, Gillian called. Well, it was all Brian's fault. Him and his dopey blind date. Speaking of which . . . Colleen glanced at the clock. She had thirty-five minutes to change clothes and get over to the restaurant.

"Smokey," she called again as she headed to her tiny kitchen. Still no sign of the errant cat. Fine, he could just wait until later for dinner.

She turned on the television to hear the tail end of the early news. As she rummaged through her closet, she thought she heard a plaintive meow. The noise from the TV distracted her. There. She heard the meow again. Where was that damn cat? Just as she reached to turn down the volume, a news story caught her ear.

"An autopsy has confirmed that porn queen Amber Rose died from an overdose of heroin. Rose was in Southeast Washington filming her new video, *Bad Moon Rising*. Her body was found late last week in her trailer by another actress. The police have yet to determine if foul play was involved. In other news . . ."

Colleen sat back on her heels and turned the sound off. The photo that had accompanied the story had intrigued her. The dead woman certainly didn't look like a porn star. Not that Colleen had personal knowledge of what porn stars looked like. She hadn't even known that such movies were filmed here in the Nation's capital. Well, Southeast did have kind of a sleazy reputation. Drugs and violence were a daily occurrence there, although the local residents were trying to turn it around. It also happened to be where the oldest lesbian bar in D.C. was located. Colleen had been to The Phase One many times, enjoying the old-time ambiance and butch-femme dynamic that played out every weekend night.

Yes, Amber Rose certainly hadn't looked like what Colleen imagined a porn star would look like. Pretty, in a Christie Brinkley sort of way, she appeared fairly young, maybe mid-twenties, with abundant wheat-blonde curls falling below her shoulders. Bright eyes, most probably blue, and a full laughing mouth showed a woman happy with life. Colleen wondered what would make a woman turn to such a living. Even if she was literally starving, Colleen was positive she would never use sex to support herself. But then again, one never knew what destitution might prompt one to do.

Another faint meow swept Amber Rose from Colleen's thoughts. The sound seemed to be coming from under the couch, but it didn't have any crawlspace underneath. "Smokey," she called. Again, the meow. Could it be? No. It couldn't possibly . . .

Colleen unfolded the couch. Sure enough, her Russian Blue was caught among the coils. She'd folded him up inside this morning when she put the bed away. He must have knocked over the phone and answering machine while clawing to get out. She could only guess how. She cradled the squirming cat in her arms.

"Poor kitty, let me feed you," she said soothingly, but he leapt out of her arms and tromped off to the bathroom.

Thank god I don't have kids, she thought as she poured extra food in Smokey's bowl. Resuming her foray through the closet, she finally settled on her new black jeans and the Norwegian sweater that had been an extravagant purchase at Epcot Center during last year's Gay Day at Disney celebration.

She gave herself one last glance in the mirror. She still wasn't used to her new haircut. The long tousled look was gone, replaced with a flattering layered cut whose longest length was barely to her shoulders. The red-gold curls looked softer now that they'd been thinned out a bit. Her skin was pale, as if dusted with rice powder, the summer freckles faded. Big blue eyes stared out at her. She smiled. Mom and Dad had spent a fortune making her teeth perfect — braces, bonding, the works. Just because she'd been in a couple of school plays, they'd had some idea about her becoming an actress. It was nice they'd had such faith in her. She wondered sometimes if they were disappointed.

She looked at the clock. It was six already. Brian would be annoyed that she was late. She gave Smokey a last once-over to be sure he'd suffered no ill effects, then she ran out the door.

Walking briskly, she made it to Food for Thought in twenty minutes. As usual, a line of people waited for tables, but Brian already sat in a booth. She waved to him and worked her way past the crowd. She slid into the seat next to him and gave him a big hug.

"You're late," he said by way of greeting.

13

"Sorry, but Smokey had a little problem." She didn't elaborate, knowing better than to give Brian ammunition for future teasing.

"Hi," Colleen said to his female companion, "I'm Colleen."

"Jenna," the woman replied huskily and nodded. "Brian's talked a lot about you."

Colleen could just imagine what sorts of things he might have told her. She fidgeted in her seat and gave a slight smile. Why had she agreed to dinner? She felt really awkward.

They fell silent as they perused the menu. Colleen knew it by heart and used the opportunity to check out the woman across from her. Brian certainly knew her type. Jenna was obviously an athlete — broad-shouldered and muscular. A swimmer perhaps? Her dark hair was cut short, almost too short. She had high cheekbones in a squarish face, a full mouth, and dark brown eyes that looked up and caught Colleen staring. Colleen felt her cheeks flush, and quickly returned her attention to the menu. She could tell it was going to be a long night.

A couple of hours later, Colleen waved to Brian and Jenna as she entered her building. The dinner had turned out to be quite pleasant after all. Jenna's rapier wit matched Brian's, and Colleen had enjoyed their playful sparring. And she had to admit, it had been fun to flirt. Jenna had made it very obvious that she liked Colleen. She was sure Jenna would have kissed her goodnight if Brian hadn't insisted on walking her home too.

As she got ready for bed, she wondered briefly if she would have invited Jenna in.

Chapter Two

"Where do you think you're going?"

Colleen looked up in surprise. "Lisa! What are you doing here this late? Isn't this your day to leave early?"

Lisa Anderson was planning an extravagant wedding, and Wednesday was the day she usually met with her wedding consultant. The big date was November 7, a little less than four weeks away.

Lisa shook her head. "Mr. Rhoades isn't quite as accommodating as Mr. Sampson was. He kept me in a meeting all afternoon, even though he knew I had to leave. Lots of stuff going on with the reorganization and all."

Colleen smiled. Lisa had gotten a promotion out of the whole mess. She was now in charge of junior investigators, of which Colleen was one.

"Want to walk out together?"

Lisa gave her a rueful smile. "The only place you're walkin' is to Mr. Rhoades' office."

Colleen couldn't help but look at her watch. "It's almost five. This can't wait until morning?" She stopped talking, thinking about how whiny she must sound. Not a good thing to do in front of a new supervisor. And it wasn't as if she had some great plans for the evening. She shrugged an apology.

"Would a new assignment make you feel better?"

"A new assignment? Like a real one? Investigating, and all that?"

Lisa smiled and ran her hands over her slim hips. It was a distracting habit that drove Colleen crazy, especially because those hips were usually encased in a mini-skirt that also showed off legs too perfect to be believed. Today was no exception. Colleen wondered if Lisa would wear a white mini to her wedding. Too late, she realized that Lisa was talking to her.

"Sorry. What did you say?"

"Where's your mind, girl? Hot date?"

Colleen tried to smile. Evading questions about her personal life was really annoying, but she just wasn't ready to come out on the job yet. Who knew how Lisa and the others would react?

"I wish," was all she said.

"Well, don't worry," Lisa gushed, "you're going to

16

have your pick of cute guys at my wedding. All my fiance's frat brothers are coming!"

"That's just great," Colleen lied.

Lisa looked at her watch. "Well, take your detour to Mr. Rhoades' office. You're officially off of desk duty now. I'd tell you about the case myself, but Mr. Rhoades said he'd do it to make up for keeping me so late today."

"Thanks, Lisa," Colleen said to Lisa's retreating backside. And a nice one it was, too. Colleen shook her head. She'd been too long without Gillian. And last evening's dinner with Brian's attractive friend had certainly whetted her sexual appetite. Jenna was smart, funny, and very attentive. Colleen remembered how the woman's bold dark eyes had sized her up and how the resulting smile of approval had brightened her handsome face.

A coworker's shouted "Good night!" jarred Colleen from her reverie. She grabbed her briefcase and headed to the meeting.

She passed through the glass doors leading to the executive suite. The two secretaries had already left. Kevin Sampson's office remained closed, but Cranford Rhoades was in his. His voice carried all the way out the partially closed door. "I don't care how much it costs, you buy him out!"

He slammed the phone down just as Colleen pushed the door open. As she hesitated, he motioned for her to come in. She sat in a leather chair identical to the one she'd sat in almost four months ago when Mr. Sampson had assigned her the Candy Emerson case. In fact, the entire office seemed identical to Sampson's, having the same panoramic view of the Potomac River, the same oak desk, even the same new wallpaper.

But Cranford Rhoades was Laurel to Kevin Sampson's Hardy. Whereas Kevin was hugely fat, Cranford was thin as a sapling. Sandy blonde hair complemented a complexion so perfectly tanned it could only have come from a tanning salon. Eyes as blue and clear as a spring sky rivaled Paul Newman's own. His designer suit fitted him as if tailor-made, and the white shirt was crisp and spotless, finished off with a dark blue tie. Suit and shirt looked just put on — not a wrinkle anywhere. Colleen was in awe. If she didn't know any better, she'd swear the man was gay. She looked at his hands — small and perfectly manicured, and decorated with a simple gold circlet on one finger. Of course, a wedding band these days didn't necessarily mean heterosexually married.

"How are you today, Miss Fitzgerald?" he asked as he extracted a folder from under some papers. His tone was smooth and cultured.

"Fine, thank you, Mr. Rhoades."

"Good. Now, I've gotten good reports about you from Miss Anderson. I realize too that you did an excellent job on your first assignment. Very impressive. Must have been exciting."

"I was just glad to uncover the truth." If you only knew just how exciting, she added silently and smiled, thinking of Gillian, whom she had yet to call back.

"Yes, nasty business. Murdering people. And all that mess with Kevin Sampson. Who would have thought? Well, I know you've been twiddling your thumbs doing all sorts of mundane things.

18

Everything's settled now with the partnership, so I think we can assign you something new."

Colleen could barely contain her excitement. Finally! "I'd like that very much," she replied.

Rhoades gave a cursory glance to the papers in the folder before he handed them to her. "We have something a little dirty here. Don't mind a little scandal, do you?"

"No, sir."

"A movie studio has filed a claim with Franklin and Associates. Seems one of their stars overdosed on heroin right in the middle of filming. The actress was modestly insured and Franklin just wants to make sure there's nothing funny here. Just do the same good job you did on the Emerson case."

A film star overdosing on heroin? It had to be the same story from the news. She looked at the top paper. The claim was on a Sheila Cunningham, thirty years old. So it wasn't the porn star.

"This is so weird," Colleen couldn't help but saying. "I just heard a news story last night about an actress OD'ing on heroin, and here's another one. Is there some kind of bad stuff out on the street?"

Rhoades gave her a funny look. "Stuff?"

She gave a nervous laugh. "Just thinking out loud, Mr. Rhoades. Thanks. I'll do my best."

He nodded his dismissal. She fairly flew out of the office. She was already thinking about what police connections she might have. Maybe Officer David Perry, whom she had met in Rehoboth on the Candy Emerson case and who had ended up saving her life, could pull some professional courtesy and connect her up with someone in the D.C. police department? She could hardly wait to tell Gillian about her new assignment.

Rather than stay at work any longer, Colleen put the file in her briefcase. It would certainly make more interesting reading than the usually badly written reports of her colleagues.

When she got to her apartment, a purring Smokey greeted her at the door. "Ah, so all has been forgiven, huh boy?" She'd been extra careful this morning when she folded up her bed. She often wished she could move into an apartment with a separate bedroom so she could have a real bed, but she knew she was lucky to be able to afford the studio apartment she did have. And the small place had become home to her in the nine or so months she'd lived there. She no longer envied her brother, William, his big suburban home and all its responsibilities. Whenever she missed having a yard, she'd go to her parents' house and mow theirs. That was enough to kill the urge right then. Just like being around her hyperkinetic nieces and nephews killed any urge she might have to have children.

Her answering machine light wasn't blinking today. She fed Smokey, threw a frozen dinner into the microwave, and stripped off her work clothes. She was so engrossed in the case file on Sheila Cunningham, she didn't even hear the microwave beep.

It turned out that Sheila and Amber Rose were one and the same. The photo on the news must have been an earlier one — maybe one of those Glamour Shots things. The film company, Starlight Studios, Inc., had rented an empty warehouse in Southeast to shoot its next release, *Bad Moon Rising*. Colleen could only venture a guess as to what the video was about with a title like that. It was only one in a series of videos being shot in D.C. The video's producer, Jackson Ramses — oh please, where did these people come up with these names? — had taken out a standard insurance policy for all of his actors. In the event any of them could not complete the video for any reason, he would get $100,000 on that actor.

Colleen wondered how many actors would be in such a video. Four or five? It couldn't have much of a plot. These types of movies never did. Not that Colleen watched them. When she was in high school, she and a bunch of friends had skipped school to sneak into a theater that still showed XXX films. She'd been so grossed out she couldn't stay but maybe fifteen minutes. It was one of the many things that helped her realize she could never sleep with men, and by the time she was twenty, she knew for sure she was a lesbian.

The file contained the official police report, as much as they knew anyway. The death had only occurred six days ago. The news brief had mentioned an autopsy. It certainly had been performed pretty quickly. Quite a feat, for this city anyway. Horribly backlogged, the City Morgue had recently made front page news as an unsavory conglomeration of rats, roaches, and slowly rotting corpses.

Sheila — or did she prefer Amber? — was found on the floor of her trailer by a fellow actress who'd gone to see why she hadn't returned from her break. Drug paraphernalia was in plain view. The medical examiner made his preliminary judgment that she'd overdosed, which was confirmed by the autopsy.

Heroin was Sheila's drug of choice, and she'd injected an almost pure dose of it.

Colleen laid the file on her lap. This case seemed pretty cut and dried to her. The insurance benefit wasn't overly large. All the other actors were insured for the same amount. No next of kin on the policy; it was strictly business. And the suicide clause common to most policies didn't apply here. Well, the insurance company must have some reason for wanting Sampson and Rhoades to check it out. That would be her first task in the morning — to find out exactly why Franklin and Associates was suspicious.

Colleen reviewed the file carefully. Other than her last-known permanent address, it contained no personal information about Sheila. Colleen was surprised to recognize it as being in the exclusive McLean area of Virginia, home to the Kennedys and other such prominent families. That would make for an interesting excursion. The closest she'd ever been to that part of Virginia was the Tysons Corner Mall.

Once again, Colleen found herself wondering why a woman like Sheila would become a porn actress. She was young — only three years older than Colleen — beautiful, and, if the McLean address was any indication, privileged. She wondered if Sheila still had any local friends. She'd probably gone to a private high school; it would be easy enough to find out which one. Still, she'd have graduated almost twelve years ago. Given her circumstances, it didn't seem likely Sheila would have kept in touch with her classmates. And had she attended college?

Smokey jumped up on the couch and climbed onto Colleen's lap. The papers crackled underneath him. She absently petted him as she batted different ideas about. She didn't really have enough information to form any kind of real theory, and then she had a sudden thought. That McLean address, for all Colleen knew, could be where Sheila had worked as a housemaid or gardener or something. Maybe she didn't come from a rich family. Maybe she only moonlighted as a porn actress. Maybe she had a secret child to support.

"Yes, and maybe aliens abducted her and forced her to star in movies about anal sex," Colleen said out loud as she pushed Smokey off her lap and went to the kitchen for her forgotten dinner. Really, her imagination was going wild. And Sampson and Rhoades did not pay her to have an imagination. They paid her to track down facts.

The phone rang, startling Colleen as she swallowed another bite of tasteless macaroni and cheese. "Hello," she choked.

"Are you okay?" a familiar voice asked.

Colleen smiled. "Yes, Gillian, I'm fine. Just a noodle going down the wrong way. How are you, darling?"

"I'm fine. Think you can come up for the Sea Witch weekend?"

"I was planning to, but I've just been assigned a new case. I don't think I can get away, but you could come here. Lots of fun things happen in Washington on Halloween." The silence on the other end seemed to crackle. Colleen waited. Finally, a tentative, "Gillian?"

"Sorry, Colleen, I was really looking forward to your coming to Rehoboth. Everyone misses you. Stephan and Phillip ask about you every day."

"How is Phillip doing?"

"Better than expected. No one thought he'd live this long after Stephan brought him home from Mexico. I guess all the love and attention is doing some good. And the new drug combination seems to have boosted his immune system."

"That makes me very happy." Colleen took a deep breath. "Gillian, I think we really need to talk about some things."

Gillian suddenly sounded rushed. "I'd love to, honey, but I've got to teach a class tonight. I'm subbing for Stephan. I'll call you soon, okay?"

"Okay. Give my love to everyone."

"Goodnight, sweetie."

"Goodnight." Colleen felt almost disoriented. It was as if she and Gillian were mere casual acquaintances speaking in formal sentences and distant promises. And Gillian hadn't even asked about her new assignment.

Chapter Three

Colleen got to the office around seven the next morning. She was still upset over Gillian's seeming indifference. If her and Gillian's circumstances were reversed, Colleen knew she'd be with Gillian every minute she could. Gillian, after all, was independently wealthy; she only worked for fun. Worked? Hell, she taught an aerobics class or two at a gym in a beach resort and wrote free-lance articles for sports magazines. Colleen threw her briefcase into her chair, disgusted with herself for her sour-grapes attitude. It wasn't Gillian's fault she had money.

She made herself a pot of coffee and settled at her desk to reread the sparse file on Sheila Cunningham, a.k.a. Amber Rose. It was too early to call the insurance company or Sheila's home, but maybe someone was at the film studio already. Colleen dialed the number.

"Hello?" a groggy male voice answered.

"Good morning," she said, "my name is Colleen Fitzgerald. May I speak with someone in charge?"

"What? Do you know how early it is?"

"I'm sorry, I thought you'd be filming already."

"Are you the replacement?"

"Replacement?"

"Yeah, you know. For the actress who got killed."

Colleen noted the choice of words. "No, I'm not the replacement, but I am an investigator looking into Amber's death."

"An investigator, huh?"

"Yes. Do you have time to talk?"

There was a moment of hesitation. "Yeah. Yeah, sure."

"And you are . . ."

"Bob Jones, the production assistant. Listen, you caught me at a bad time. Give me half an hour, and I'll get back to you."

Colleen gave him her phone number and hung up. She wrote his name and job title on a new page in a new notebook. Jones' words about Amber's death were interesting. Colleen jotted them down too. If she was lucky, he would be a good lead as to what really happened. She naively wondered just how common it was for porn actresses to die from heroin overdoses.

She spent the next hour searching through computer files. Starlight Studios mostly used

Cincinnati-based Franklin and Associates to insure its employees, including the temporary ones. They'd only filed claims on four others over a six-year period — a cameraman died of a heart attack, two extras died in a car accident unrelated to filming, and an actor was murdered by his ex-girlfriend. That certainly didn't seem like a suspicious trend.

Colleen searched further and found that during that same six-year period, Starlight had insured with Berger and Sons out of New York, who'd dropped them after a fire destroyed an entire production — sets, costumes, film, and equipment. Three people had died in that blaze. Colleen blinked when she saw the seven-figure amount paid out. She was sure the insurance company must have suspected arson, but the final report had no proof of that. No wonder Berger had dropped them — and no wonder Franklin and Associates wanted this case checked out.

Colleen decided to go on the Web and see if Starlight had a homepage. They did, and she was amazed to see they'd had almost a quarter million hits. The page was easy to read with a catchy logo and good use of colors. Starlight had obviously had a professional design it. Several clicks later, Colleen found what she was looking for, a listing of all of Amber Rose's videos.

Each video was cleverly advertised with a full-color photo, the video's title, and some teasing copy. A topless Amber crawled out of a doghouse for *Backdoor Bitches*. A bound Amber and two brawny men in American Indian garb for *Pocahotass*. Amber naked in a huge champagne glass for *Bottoms Up*. Colleen thought of making a list of all the actors in the videos so she could cross-reference them with drug-related deaths, but as she read through cast lists that included "Honey Suckle," "Ben Dover," and "Hugh E. Rection," she realized that none of these people worked under their real names. As she scrolled down the page, a notice appeared telling her she'd need to buy a membership to see "more explicit" photos. Having seen enough, Colleen clicked on the merchandise icon and up popped offers for posters, calendars, coffee mugs, and autographed photos of "Amber in Action." They even hawked pairs of Amber's "just worn panties — complete with certificate of authenticity! Only $49.94!!!"

The phone startled her. "Fitzgerald here."

"You the one who called earlier about Amber?"

"Yes, Mr. Jones. Can you talk now?"

"I'd rather meet you somewhere."

Not sure who she was dealing with, Colleen picked a safe place in a well-populated area. "Do you know the Starbucks on DuPont Circle?"

"I'll find it. Be there in half an hour."

He hung up so abruptly, she stared at the phone in surprise. He hadn't even asked what she looked like. This whole thing was beginning to feel like a bad spy movie, and she'd only just started the investigation.

After signing off her computer, Colleen made a list of the people she needed to call, then left the office. She took the subway back to DuPont Circle and arrived at Starbucks five minutes early. The place was crowded with morning commuters, but after buying a cappuccino, she managed to find a seat that gave her a good view of the door. She had no idea what Bob Jones looked like, so she scrutinized each

28

man who came through the door. The appointed time came and went. Finally, about twenty minutes later, a short squat man dressed in jeans and a leather jacket came in and glanced around the room as if looking for someone. She rose and approached him.

"Bob Jones?"

"Yeah. You Fitzgerald?"

"I've got a table over here," she said by way of reply.

He bought a cup of coffee and then joined her. For a few minutes, they were silent. He was a burly man with shoulders like football pads. He obviously worked out, and looked more to her like a bar bouncer than a production assistant. The round, sunburnt face sported light brown eyes, a crooked nose, a five o'clock shadow, and a surprisingly feminine mouth. A crewcut made it difficult to determine his hair color. The hands that held the coffee cup were big and gnarly, with fingernails bitten to the quick.

"So, what does a production assistant do?" she asked, to break the ice.

"Little bit of everything. Build the sets, rig the lights, take care of the, uh, props." He looked at her a little sheepishly. "Someone's gotta make sure things run smoothly, ya know?"

Colleen nodded and smiled in a way she hoped would encourage him to trust her. "Is there some reason why you didn't want to meet at the studio? I would have liked to have seen it."

He glanced nervously around the room. "Don't want no trouble. People get nervous when you talk to the cops."

Colleen raised her eyebrows. "But I'm not with the police. My investigation is routine with insurance claims." She handed him her card.

"Look, I just don't want no one gettin' any wrong ideas, okay? Amber was a good kid. It's just not right what happened to her."

"It's not that uncommon for a drug addict to overdose."

He took a big gulp of coffee. "Just between you and me, I don't think she OD'd. The cops, they're too eager to accept that. I mean, that heroin was, like, pure. Uncut. The chances of a drug dealer screwing up like that are slim to none."

"What do you mean?"

"These dealers. They usually 'cut' the stuff to make it go further on the street. Sometimes you have to worry more about dying from what they've added to it than the drug itself." He took a swallow of coffee. "No, someone went to a lot of trouble to make it look like Amber did it herself."

Colleen hid her surprise. "Are you saying that someone else injected Amber with the heroin?"

He shook his head. "See, Amber wasn't no skin-poppin' club kid. She's been mainlining for as long as I've known her. What I'm sayin' is, she knew exactly how much to shoot. I think someone planted the pure stuff."

"Well, who do you think gave it to her?"

"I wouldn't put it past that scumbag Jackson. He'd been treatin' her real bad lately. Callin' her an ugly, washed-out whore and stuff like that, ya know? He kept talkin' about replacing her with a younger girl. They had a big fight right before she went to her trailer."

"You're talking about Jackson Ramses?"

"Yeah."

"What did they fight about?"

"He was always raggin' on her. You name it, he complained about it. Her weight. Her hair. The way she sucked dick."

His last sentence seemed to echo throughout the staid coffee bar. Colleen tried to look cool. She glanced around and noted a woman at the next table looking back disapprovingly. That's what you get for eavesdropping, Colleen thought. She sat back in her chair and took a sip of cappuccino. Bob was also glancing around the room. He looked ready to bolt at any minute.

"Have you talked to the police about this?"

He gave a snort of disgust. "I told 'em. They're not interested. It's not like she was stabbed or anything. To them she's just an addict. And a porn star." He let out a hollow laugh.

"What's so funny?"

"Know what they asked me when I tried to talk to them?" He didn't wait for Colleen to respond. "The bastards wanted some free videos." He shook his head and stood up. "Listen, I gotta go."

"Wait. Was Jackson the only one she had trouble with?"

He paused, as if deep in thought. "These girls, they all have trouble with wankers, ya know?" Colleen's blank expression must have told him she didn't know. "Wackos that follow them around. One guy especially. He was always sniffin' around, trying to see Amber. He'd send her things — some of them kind of sick."

"What do you mean 'sick'?"

31

Bob grimaced. "One time he sent her a jar of cum ... I mean, semen. I seen a lot of stuff in this business, but this guy takes the cake. His name's Rick Ewing. He always included his name and phone number with his presents."

"Any others who hung around regularly?"

"Just the protesters. Women's libbers and religious nuts, ya know? I'm sure you'll run into them if you come by the studio."

"One more question, please? Did you know Amber had family in the area?"

"She mentioned her dad once in a while. Said he was some bigwig living out in Virginia somewhere. I figured she was bullshittin'. Some of the girls do that, ya know. Make up stories about where they come from and all. Kinda sad, really."

Colleen stood and offered her hand. He took it briefly in a firm grip. "Can I call you again?" she asked.

"Sure. I'm stayin' at the studio."

He was gone before she could say another word. She pulled out her notebook and added what Bob had told her to his earlier comments. Personally, she thought he was grasping at straws, unable to deal with Amber's death for whatever reasons of his own. On impulse, she put Bob's name on a page labeled "Suspects," along with Rick Ewing's. If Bob had some obsession with her, he could have had his own reasons to want her dead. He did seem to know a lot about her drug habit. She bit her lip in frustration. She hadn't thought to ask him if he knew Amber's supplier. She'd bet a week's salary that he did.

She finished her cappuccino and headed back to the office. Her first call was to Franklin and

32

Associates. They told her they merely wanted to make sure there was nothing unusual with the claim. They always got a little nervous when someone filed numerous claims, and this was Starlight's fifth one. Next she called information to get a phone number for Sheila's father. The Cunninghams in McLean had an unlisted number. No amount of cajoling would entice the operator to give her the number, so she decided it was time to enlist the help of her friend — and lifesaver — Officer David Perry. It would give her an excuse to call Gillian.

She took the photo from its hiding place as she dialed the phone. Gillian's face smiled up at her, and then her low voice sent tingles up Colleen's spine.

"What a nice surprise."

"I'm glad you think so. I need your help with something. Could you get me David's phone number?"

"You don't have it?"

Colleen most certainly did, but she told a white lie. "Lost it."

Gillian gave her his home number, as well as that of the Rehoboth police station. "What's this all about?"

"I just want him to use his authority to get a phone number for me. It's this new case I'm on. Would you believe I'm investigating the death of a porn star?"

Gillian's deep-throated laugh made Colleen wish they were in bed together. Gillian gave a whole new meaning to the phrase "breakfast in bed." Was Colleen making a mistake by insisting on staying in Washington? It was becoming more obvious to her that Gillian didn't want to leave Rehoboth.

"That must be interesting," Gillian commented.

"It is. Seems the woman came from money. How one Sheila Cunningham of McLean, Virginia, ended up as porn star Amber Rose should be an enlightening story."

Gillian's gasp on the other end of the phone took Colleen by surprise. "Gillian? Are you okay?"

"I don't believe it. Sheila Cunningham? From McLean? Are you serious?"

"You *know* her?" More silence. "Gillian?"

"I don't want to talk about this on the phone. I'll be there this afternoon."

Chapter Four

Colleen stared at the phone. She'd been wanting Gillian to come to Washington, and now she'd be here between two and three. But what in God's name was her connection to Sheila? Was it even the same Sheila Cunningham? The only way to keep from going crazy until Gillian arrived was to stay busy. She made her call to David, who called back soon after with the information she needed. A call to the McLean address only revealed that Mr. Cunningham was unavailable due to a death in the family. A quick review of the *Washington Post* obits revealed that

Sheila's funeral would take place that day. At least it confirmed that she probably had the right Cunningham. She left her name and number, not really expecting a call back.

She decided she wanted to talk to Jackson Ramses. The problem was getting to the studio. Even if she found a taxi driver who agreed to take her to Southeast, it was doubtful she'd find one to bring her back. Although it was illegal for cab drivers to refuse service to that part of the city, it happened all the time. That meant she'd have to drive herself, which entailed yet another trip back to DuPont Circle to pick up her car.

The only time she drove her almost new raspberry-red Saturn was when she had to leave the city or when she visited The Phase One. She consulted her map, then regretfully pulled out of her great parking space, which she knew would be gone by the time she returned.

With rush hour over and few tourists around, she made it across town to the warehouse in only twenty minutes. The flat-roofed, two-story building looked old and deserted, its red brick faded and windows blackened out. The cargo bays where trucks once unloaded their wares stood empty. She didn't see protesters, or anyone else for that matter.

The parking lot was in bad shape, rutted and full of potholes. Grass sprouted between cracks in the pavement. Colleen parked her car near a new BMW with temporary tags. Four old trailers were clustered near the south end of the lot. She walked over. They all had crude gold stars on the doors. One had the remnants of police tape fluttering in the slight wind. Without seeing the name handwritten on the faded gold star, Colleen knew it was Amber's trailer. She walked up the steps and grasped the doorknob.

"Hey! What do you think you're doing?"

Colleen turned. A tall, well-dressed, rather handsome man came striding over, anger in every step. Before she could answer, he yelled again.

"We've had enough curiosity-seekers around here. You're trespassing. Now, get out!"

She descended the steps and pulled out her identification, which he examined closely then handed back with an apology.

"It's understandable," Colleen said. "I'm here to see Mr. Ramses."

"That's me," he said, extending his hand. "Please, come to my office."

She followed him into the warehouse, looking around with interest. The blackened windows made it dark inside, the bare bulbs on the walls casting a feeble light along the seemingly endless corridor. Doors on the left side were closed. Colleen and Jackson's footsteps on the concrete floor echoed eerily behind them. Finally, he opened one of the doors, and she found herself in an area almost the size of a football field. Skylights made the brightness almost blinding after the gloom of the corridor. She blinked several times to adjust her eyes to the light.

She blinked again when she looked in the very center of the room. Cameras and bright lamps surrounded a king-size bed draped with black sheets, upon which three people were having sex. Two women bent their heads over one man. He was naked; the women wore only garters with stockings and high heels. A dark-haired woman alternated between kissing the man's mouth and chest. The other woman's head bobbed up and down between his legs, her long red hair draped over his muscular thighs. Behind them and alongside the bed, two cameramen zoomed in for a close-up.

"Move the hair!" someone barked.

Colleen couldn't see who had yelled, but the redhead flipped her hair expertly behind her ear, leaving no doubt then as to what she was doing. Colleen couldn't help but gasp as another cameraman climbed onto the bed and used a hand-held camera to film what should have been a most intimate moment. Both women started moaning loudly as the man bucked his hips and ejaculated all over the redhead's face. The dark-haired woman leaned over and started licking it off.

Grimacing, Colleen averted her eyes and quickly followed Jackson across the floor to a cubicle-sized office at the far left side of the room. She wondered briefly where Bob Jones worked. She'd seen no sign of him in the studio.

Jackson closed the door and motioned to a chair across from his gray metal desk. Colleen sat speechless, still thinking about what she had just seen. While the thought of heterosexual sex per se didn't bother her too much, blow job scenes were much too disgusting for her taste.

"So, you're here about Amber. Any problems?"

Struggling to compose herself, Colleen took out her notebook. How could he be so nonchalant, she wondered as she cleared her throat nervously. "Your insurance company just wants us to check things out. Nothing out of the ordinary."

"Shame about Amber. She was one of my best girls."

"Did you know about her drug problem?"

He didn't look at her when he answered. "Course not."

She knew he was lying, but she was more interested in finding out about his argument with Amber. "I heard that you and Amber had been having problems lately."

"Nothing more than usual. I'm a film producer. Sometimes producers and talent have ... What should I call it? Creative differences. I didn't think Amber was performing well."

"What do you mean?"

"She was lethargic, couldn't remember her lines."

Colleen couldn't help but smile. Just how many lines would Amber have to memorize? "Did you have a fight the day of her death?"

"No, not a fight. An argument. She just wasn't doing the job. I told her to take a break. She never came back. I sent Tiffany to get her, and she came back all hysterical. It wasn't a pretty sight."

"Tiffany is another actress?"

"Yeah, Tiffany Glass." He gave a big guffaw. "What a name, eh? My idea. Her real name's Judith Weinberg. She's the dark-haired one out there."

"I'd like to speak with her later, if you don't mind. Actually, I'd like to speak to everyone in the studio. How many employees do you have?"

He raised his eyes to the ceiling and moved his lips silently. Then he looked back at her. "On this video, we've got eleven. Only five in the cast."

"Was Amber depressed?"

"Not that I could tell. What is depression these days?"

Colleen made a big show of consulting her notes. "Who is Rick Ewing?"

Jackson looked at her with a frown. "Sounds like you've been talking to people already. Rick's just a crazy fan. He followed us out here from California. Thought Amber belonged to him. Didn't like her being with the other men. We finally had to get a restraining order against him, but he still manages to sneak around. Now that Amber's dead, it doesn't matter."

"You don't think he might have had something to do with her death?"

"I don't think he injected her with the heroin, if that's what you're getting at. Besides, I didn't see him around that day. Only the protesters."

"Were they hostile?"

Jackson shrugged. "No more than usual. Let's see, that day we had the Feminazi lawyer and her crew — about four of them — and Randy Wilson. Wilson's quite a character. Used to be in porn videos himself, but he contracted HIV, then become born again. Now he's waging a one-man war against the industry."

Colleen didn't like Jackson's use of the term "Feminazi." He'd been listening to too much Rush Limbaugh. "And the feminist lawyer, what's her name?"

"Jenna Bolden."

Colleen looked up with a start. Jenna Bolden? The woman Brian had set her up with Tuesday night? Talk about a small world. Well, at least she'd be easy to track down.

"You said Ewing 'followed' you out here from California. Is that where you usually work?"

"Yeah, but a friend of mine works for the city, and he promised all sorts of tax breaks if I shot some films here. It was a nice chance for a change of scene."

After questioning Ramses in more depth about the insurance policy and the circumstances of Amber's death, she snapped her notebook shut. "I think that's all for now, Mr. Ramses. When's a good time for me to talk to the others?"

He looked at his watch. "I'll call an early lunch. Give them a half-hour to wrap up the shoot. You can stay here in my office . . ." He gave her a lewd grin. "Or, you can come watch . . ."

Colleen felt herself blushing. "I'll stay here, if you don't mind. Could I use the phone?"

He scraped his chair back and stood up. "Of course."

She breathed a sigh of relief when he left. She didn't know how to read the man. He surprised her with his extraordinarily good looks and friendly manner. She was aware that she was letting her presumptions influence her first impressions. Why couldn't someone be nice and handsome *and* into porn too? Pornography, or erotica, depending on your point of view, was no longer some slimy back-alley production.

She looked around the small office. No photos on the walls or the desk. Everything was pretty sparse. Surreptitiously, she rose from her chair and approached the filing cabinet. A quick tug revealed it to be locked. She'd expected no less. Keeping an eye on the window in the door, she shuffled the papers

41

on the desk, hoping to find the key there. The desk drawer was partially open. She glanced at her watch, then pulled the drawer open all the way. A key rested on top of some paper clips in a plastic container. She smiled as it opened the cabinet.

Files were stacked neatly by last name. Sheila's folder was in the front, filed under Cunningham instead of Rose. She shuffled through the file, noting with interest two photocopies of picture I.D.'s. Curiously, Sheila'd had driver's licenses from both California and Virginia. Colleen wished she had one of those tiny cameras that always showed up in spy movies. She'd barely been able to read the first page of the file when she caught sight of Jackson coming toward the office. She hastily stuffed the folder back, locked the cabinet, and replaced the key. She'd just sat back in her chair when he opened the door.

"Everyone is decent. You can come out now."

Did she detect a note of sarcasm in his voice? "Nudity does not offend me," she said, more to quash any opinions he might have of her than because it was the truth.

"Nor should it," he replied.

In the big room, the three video stars casually sat on the big bed. The redhead sat alone on one side, smoking a cigarette. The other woman and the man, so much alike they could be related, sat on the other side, laughing at some private joke. They all wore robes now. The two cameramen lounged in folding chairs. Four other people she hadn't seen before stood nearby, clearly nervous. She still had seen nothing of Bob Jones.

"This is Miss Fitzgerald on behalf of Franklin and Associates. She has some questions she'd like to ask you about Amber's death. I told her you'd all cooperate to the fullest. We have nothing to hide."

He backed away and smiled at her. Colleen smiled back, wondering what he'd said to them before. His little speech was obviously for her benefit. As nine pairs of eyes scrutinized her, she felt like a prisoner in a police lineup.

"I'll be glad to talk to you as a group, but I'd like to interview each of you individually also. Perhaps Mr. Ramses would let us use his office?" She glanced at him.

He looked annoyed. "How long is this going to take? Amber's death has already put us behind schedule. Her replacement isn't quite ready yet."

She changed her tactic. "We'll do without the individual interviews for now. However," she said as she handed out business cards, "if any of you feel you'd like to talk privately, you may call me at my office."

The redhead spoke first. "There was nothing funny in Amber's death, if that's what you're looking for. She was a junkie who OD'd on smack. End of story."

"Was she depressed? Fighting with anyone?"

One or two of the people glanced at Jackson. "Nothing out of the ordinary," a cameraman answered.

"Can I get all of your names, please? Your real ones."

Colleen wrote them down, each person receiving a new page in her notebook. None of them really had much to say, at least not in front of the others. Colleen was sure she would be receiving a call from at least one or two of them. The redhead, Julia

Osborne, seemed a likely candidate, as did one of the cameramen, Lance Lawson. Both of them avoided looking at her, while glancing continuously at Jackson. Julia smoked nonstop during the short half-hour that Colleen questioned the crew.

She finally snapped the notebook shut, as eager to leave as they were to have her leave.

"You've all been a big help," she lied. "If you think of anything else, please call me." She turned to Jackson. "Thanks for your time. I know you're on a tight schedule."

He took her proffered hand and gave her a dazzling smile. "Anytime." He was back to his charming self.

"I'll find my way out." Colleen wanted the chance to snoop a little.

"No," Jackson was quick to say, "I'll walk with you." He turned to the others. "Break's over."

Colleen hid her disappointment as they retraced their way to the outside. Again their footsteps echoed through the long corridor. They exited into the bright sun. Colleen had to blink several times.

"Thanks again, Mr. Ramses." She turned to go, then turned back again. "By the way, I did speak to everyone on your crew?"

"Yup."

"I thought you said there were eleven people on the payroll?"

"Yeah. You talked to nine and then there's me and the new girl." His tone had become a little less charming.

She walked slowly to her car. As she got in, she

saw that Jackson still stood in the doorway. She was certain he was making sure that she didn't take a side trip to any of the trailers on the lot, especially Amber's. As she drove away, she made a mental note to call Brian at Lambda Rising. She needed Jenna's phone number.

Chapter Five

Gillian Smith hurriedly stuffed clothes into an Army duffel bag. She couldn't believe that her college friend and sweetheart, Sheila Cunningham, was dead. Or that Sheila had gotten involved in pornography. She'd been so beautiful, talented, and smart. An aerospace engineering major at N.Y.U., Sheila had talked about becoming the first out lesbian astronaut. The memory made Gillian smile.

She threw the last item into the bag and zipped it up. Glancing around the luxurious hotel room that had been home to her since her father's death, she thought briefly that it was time she found something more permanent. Colleen had been wanting her to move to D.C. for weeks. What prevented her? Rehoboth was only a short three- to four-hour drive from the city, depending on traffic. The friends she'd made in the beach resort town wouldn't be lost or forgotten. She cared deeply about Colleen, but was it love? Gillian's love for bodybuilder Candy Emerson had been stronger than any she'd felt before, and her murder had been almost too much to bear. Colleen was the one woman who'd been able to make her feel again. But how would Colleen react to the news that Gillian knew Sheila? Knew her? Hell, she'd been crazy about her.

Gillian locked the door and took the elevator to the parking garage. She hadn't driven the Mercedes since the last time she'd visited Colleen and hoped it would start okay.

Driving out of Rehoboth, Gillian thought of Sheila — blonde, pretty, laughing Sheila. She'd come from a wealthy family too and, like Gillian, had entered N.Y.U. out of defiance, rejecting her parents' wish for an Ivy League school. Sheila had been so out, unlike Gillian, who struggled with her sexuality following a brief, hot-tempered affair with a female rugby player. Sheila had taken it upon herself to help Gillian through the rough waters.

The first time she'd seen Sheila, Gillian had been sitting in a deep, dark corner of the university library when a commotion drew her attention from a tome on the history of the English language. The tall woman who had dropped her books looked like she had stepped from the pages of a surfer magazine. Tanned and blonde, the calendar-perfect California girl, she had Caribbean blue eyes that caught Gillian's gaze and held her like a bunny caught in headlights. The radiant smile was deadly. Gillian was lost.

Sheila picked up her books and sashayed over to Gillian's table. "This seat taken?" she'd asked in a voice as melodic as a Strauss waltz.

Gillian could only shake her head. The blonde vision sat down and proceeded to introduce herself. By the end of the afternoon, Sheila had somehow gotten Gillian to reluctantly admit that she liked women, and they had a date for Saturday night. The affair — it couldn't be called anything else — had lasted the rest of the year and ended as explosively as it had started. By then, Gillian was confident in her lesbianism and considered herself out, but by no means an activist. She only saw Sheila from afar during the next year or so because Sheila's in-your-face activism had scared her. Then came the phone call in the middle of the night.

"Gillian," a woman's voice pleaded, "I need you. Please meet me at the playground in the park."

"Who is this?" Gillian asked sleepily, the voice only vaguely familiar. She only heard more crying. "Sheila, is that you?"

"Yes. Oh please, meet me there. Oh god, I don't know where else to turn."

Fully awake, Gillian sat up and said, "I'm on the way."

She found Sheila huddled under the slide. She'd been severely beaten, but wouldn't let Gillian take her to the emergency room or call the police. It seemed she'd been experimenting with cocaine. A dealer she didn't know had met her in the park, raped her, beaten her, and left her for dead. She didn't want her stern father to find out.

Gillian spent the next month nursing her back to health and off the drugs the best she could. Then Sheila discovered she was pregnant. Gillian urged her to have an abortion, but she refused. Three months before the baby was due, Sheila disappeared without a trace.

Gillian tried desperately to find her, but to no avail. She'd attempted to contact Sheila's father, but he would not return her phone calls. None of their mutual friends knew anything either. She checked with hospitals and police stations. She tried to place a missing persons report, only to be told that no one but Sheila's next-of-kin had the authority to do that. Every path she took turned out to be a dead end.

Gillian knew her own life could very well have turned out just like Sheila's. She too had dabbled with drugs, spending an unauthorized vacation in Mexico getting stoned on her father's money and sleeping with every woman who would have her. When she'd finally returned to America, her father had the police waiting and she'd been arrested. Thank god that was all behind her now. Had it really been that long ago?

Lost in thought during most of the drive, Gillian arrived in D.C. with little memory of how she'd gotten there. She debated whether to go to Colleen's office or wait in her apartment. Deciding she still needed time to collect her thoughts, she opted for the apartment.

She was greeted by loud meowing the instant she slipped the key Colleen had given her into the door. The cat rubbed against her legs, seemingly happy to have a visitor in the middle of the day. Gillian gave him a cursory pat and went to the kitchen for a soda. She smiled when she saw what looked like a lifetime supply of 7UP, Colleen's favorite drink. The sound of it tumbling over the ice in her glass helped soothe her jangled nerves.

She plopped on the couch and the cat immediately jumped into her lap. What was his name? She could never remember. She wasn't really a cat person, but she absently rubbed his head. She took a long gulp of soda and dialed Colleen's office.

"Fitzgerald here."

"Hey, Colleen. It's me. I'm here."

"In the city? Where are you?"

"I'm in your apartment keeping the cat company."

Colleen laughed. It made Gillian feel good inside. "Why do you keep calling him 'the cat'? His name's Smokey."

"Listen, do you think you could get off early? I really need to talk about this case you're on." There was silence on the other end of the phone. "Colleen?" she prompted.

"Yes, I'll be home soon. I need to talk to you too."

Gillian hung up slowly. Why did she feel so uncomfortable suddenly? She certainly had nothing to do with Sheila's death. There would be no suspicion on her this time, unlike when Candy died.

Colleen hung up the phone. She should feel excited that Gillian had arrived, but somehow the excitement would not come. She didn't like that one bit.

She dialed Lambda Rising's number and Brian answered. She managed to get Jenna Bolden's home and office phone numbers from him without too much teasing, which probably meant the store was busy.

She got Jenna's secretary. After leaving a message to call, Colleen packed up her briefcase and left the office. Lisa was not at her desk when Colleen stopped by, so Colleen left a note saying she was following up on a lead in the Cunningham case. It wasn't a total lie. Gillian did have something to do with it. Colleen just didn't know what.

The key in the lock roused Gillian from her nap. She'd fallen asleep on the couch, with Smokey still in her lap. He jumped down when he heard the key and immediately started yowling. Gillian didn't understand how Colleen could put up with such a racket.

At first she didn't think the person coming through the door was Colleen after all. "You've cut your hair," she managed to say.

Colleen put her hand to her head. "Yes. I take it you don't like it."

"Of course I do," Gillian lied glibly, already missing the cascading just-out-of-bed look. She gave her a big kiss. She had to admit, it felt good to hold Colleen in her arms. They'd been apart entirely too long, and she knew she had no one to blame but herself. Their kiss was long and almost frantic. The weeks of abstinence had not been easy. "Mmmm, you feel so good."

"So do you."

51

Colleen's breath tickled Gillian's neck. At that moment, all thoughts of Sheila and everything else fled. All she could think of was ridding Colleen of her clothes and taking her right on the living room floor. As they kissed passionately, she deftly unbuttoned Colleen's black trench coat, then started on her suit. The jacket, the skirt, the white Oxford blouse — all came off in what seemed like one fluid movement. Gillian stepped back to look at Colleen standing before her, clad only in white lace and satin. The sight took her breath away. The fiery red-gold hair was still exciting, despite its shorter length. Colleen's ice-blue eyes darkened with passion, and her pale skin flushed with anticipation.

Gillian took Colleen once again into her arms. She kissed the neck so neatly exposed. There were some advantages to the shorter haircut, Gillian thought briefly as she let her mouth wander from Colleen's neck, across her shoulders, and then down to the cleavage so enticingly framed by the lace bra. Colleen moaned and grabbed Gillian's head, something that always drove Gillian wild. Her pulse racing, she allowed Colleen to push her head down. She ran her tongue along Colleen's smooth belly as she grabbed the lace underpants and pulled them down. Colleen's knees buckled as Gillian brought her tongue lower still. Gillian eased her gently to the floor. Her touch was gentle, yet firm. She let her hands travel the length of Colleen's body and brought them up again to rest on Colleen's hips. Colleen squirmed beneath her, impatient, but Gillian intended on making her wait just a little longer.

She kissed her way back up Colleen's body as she brought her hand slowly between Colleen's legs.

Colleen gasped and pushed her hips forward as Gillian's fingers fluttered over her. She was wet and ready. Colleen moaned as Gillian bit her neck and then slowly slid her tongue down Colleen's body to where her fingers teased. She inserted first one finger, then another, all the while kissing and licking the soft folds of skin between Colleen's legs. With a secret smile, Gillian lifted her head and suddenly thrust deep and hard, sending Colleen into a frenzy. Gillian nipped her neck, her shoulders, her breasts, her belly. She withdrew her fingers and knelt between Colleen's legs, lifting her easily to her mouth. Colleen grabbed her hair and pulled Gillian closer. Gillian tasted her and felt Colleen's wetness spread across her cheeks.

The muscles of her arms quivering, Gillian held Colleen up and let her tongue lick Colleen's clitoris softly and then harder, letting Colleen's movements dictate her preference. When Colleen's trembling release vibrated beneath her, only then did Gillian lower Colleen's hips to the floor.

"What do you want to do for dinner?" Colleen asked, hours later. She sat wrapped in a blanket on the couch, enjoying the warm feel of her nakedness beneath the soft wool. Stretched out on the floor, Gillian chose to remain naked. Her eyes were closed, and she smiled in a pleased sort of way. Like a cat with mischief on its mind, Colleen thought as she noticed that Gillian's body showed no tan lines.

"How about more of what we just had?" Gillian answered without opening her eyes.

"We can save that for dessert. Right now, I'm famished."

Gillian rolled over onto her side and propped herself up on one elbow. "I like making you hungry." Her voice carried just the right amount of innuendo.

Colleen got off the couch and joined her on the floor, still wrapped in the blanket. She kissed her. "If you moved to Washington you could keep me hungry all the time." She bit Gillian's neck lightly.

To her surprise, Gillian moved away from her. "Let's not talk about that now." She stood up abruptly and walked to the bathroom.

Colleen bit her lip to stop the tears. They'd just spent a wonderful afternoon making love and she wasn't going to let anything spoil it. Smokey came over and pushed against her. She stroked his fur for a few minutes, then rose and threw the blanket off. Colleen could hear the water running in the bathroom. She quickly got dressed.

Gillian emerged fully clothed, smiling as if their little moment of tension never occurred. She said, "You're dressed. Good. Let's go to that place you like over on P Street. What's it called?"

"Café Luna."

"Okay. My treat. And I want to hear all about your new case."

Colleen let Gillian help her into her jacket. It was amazing how deftly Gillian could change the subject and act as if nothing had happened, but Colleen couldn't forget about it.

Chapter Six

The walk from Colleen's apartment took them down Connecticut Avenue. The sidewalks were crowded with people taking advantage of the mild October evening. As they passed Lambda Rising, Gillian made a move to go inside, but Colleen saw Brian behind the counter.

"We'll stop by later," she said. She knew Brian would insist on joining them for dinner, and she didn't think she could put up with his incessant chatter. Besides, Gillian had just gotten into town. Colleen wasn't ready to share her with anyone yet.

Holding hands, they turned left on P Street. In this part of the city, it was not uncommon to see people of the same sex holding hands, despite the few gay-bashings that took place both in broad daylight and at night. Colleen always experienced a little nervousness, but she felt protected by Gillian, who always walked on the outside.

The café was not busy yet. The weather was mild enough to sit outside. They placed their orders, and when the drinks arrived, Gillian leaned back in her chair and smiled.

Before Gillian could say anything, Colleen spoke, "I got the distinct impression from our phone conversation that you recognized Sheila Cunningham's name. Want to tell me about it?"

"Tell me about the case first."

How like Gillian to deflect my question with one of her own, Colleen thought. "Well, she was filming a video at a warehouse in the city and appears to have overdosed on heroin. The company had her insured for a small amount of money, and I'm checking to make sure everything is on the up-and-up. Not much more than that."

"Oh, come on, Colleen. There has to be more. How could this happen? How do they know she wasn't killed?"

"Hold on a minute, Gillian. I think your involvement in Candy's murder has you seeing things that aren't there."

"That's not fair. I don't think every dead person is a murder victim." She took a sip of wine. "Okay. I did know Sheila. She just wasn't the kind of girl who'd do such a thing."

"Do what? Be a porn actress or die of a drug overdose?"

"Neither!" Her voice was loud. The other patrons looked over from their tables. She took another nervous sip of her drink. Colleen saw that her hands were shaking. It surprised her.

"Just how well did you know her?"

A flash of emotion crossed Gillian's face. Her green eyes darkened to almost black. The look of sadness was one that Colleen had only seen once before — when she'd first met Gillian after the murder of Candy Emerson. She knew then that Sheila had been as important in Gillian's life as Candy had. The thought made her very uncomfortable.

"We were college sweethearts."

"Sheila was the rugby player who brought you out?" Colleen asked incredulously. The image of the slender blonde beauty participating in such a rough sport just didn't fit.

The waiter brought their dinners. It seemed to give Gillian time to collect her thoughts. She appeared less stressed and smiled with genuine humor.

"Oh no. Sheila came after the rugby player. I was having a hard time accepting my gayness, and Sheila helped me through that. We were together only a few months, but it was very intense."

"It seems she was more of a 'sweetheart' than the rugby player. Why didn't you tell me about her?"

Gillian wouldn't meet Colleen's eyes. "I don't

know." She lifted a fork full of pasta, then put it down. "When you say pornography, do you mean hardcore?"

Remembering her session at the warehouse film studio, Colleen nodded grimly. "Tell me one thing, Gillian. I know she came from money. She's not your classic she-didn't-have-anywhere-else-to-turn case. Why would she do this?"

"I think her father disinherited her."

"Why?"

Gillian told her everything — the meeting in the library, the love affair, the frantic phone call in the middle of the night, the beating and the drugs, the pregnancy, and Sheila's disappearance. It was a lot to think about, and they ate the rest of the meal in silence.

"I intend to talk with her father," Colleen finally said. "Do you want to come with me?"

Gillian laughed bitterly. "Roger Cunningham. I'm sure he wishes I were dead too. We only met once, but it was enough for him to blame me for his daughter's lesbianism. See, I fit all the stereotypes. I was big and butch. It wasn't possible that his precious princess could have corrupted me."

"What do you do mean he wishes you were dead too? Do you think he's *glad* Sheila is dead?"

"If I know Roger, he was more upset by her sexual orientation than the fact that she starred in triple-X films. Listen, maybe I can at least drive you out to the house. I'd like to see where she grew up. Your credentials will get you in the door. Of course, if he sees me, you can forget it."

"What else can you tell me about her? Siblings? Other friends or lovers?"

"Sorry. I haven't seen or heard from Sheila since she disappeared. I don't even know if the baby was ever born. And as far as I know, she was an only child."

Colleen reached across the table and covered Gillian's hand with her own. The pain Gillian felt was evident in her voice and the way she held her body. It was as if she had pulled inside herself. Her vulnerability was something Colleen didn't know how to handle. She wanted to make Gillian feel better, but at the same time, she couldn't shake the nagging discomfort she felt at Gillian's story. She could feel doubt creep into her mind like an insect burrowing into rotting wood, and she didn't like the feeling one bit.

"Let's go home," she said.

Friday morning, Colleen woke early and left for the dreaded dental appointment. It had felt good sleeping in Gillian's arms. Afterward, she decided to visit Roger Cunningham without Gillian. She went to the office to collect her notes, and then drove out of the city into Virginia after consulting a map. The long trip around the Capital Beltway wasn't made easier by an accident-caused backup, and as she passed the exit to I-270, she remembered the dinner plans with her parents tomorrow night. Pulling out her cell phone, she called to cancel, thankful when she got their answering machine. By the time she pulled into the driveway of the Cunningham estate, she was exhausted. After taking a few moments to collect herself, she walked purposefully up the path to the steps leading to huge double doors. Twin columns guarded the enormous porch that ran the length of the whole front of the house. A butler opened the door before she could use the ornate brass knocker.

"We're not talking to the press," he said in a voice dripping with British hauteur. He ignored the hand that held her business card.

"I'm not a journalist," she replied. "I'm an insurance investigator."

He looked down his nose at her, the very epitome of a butler from a Masterpiece Theater production. "An investigator?"

"Yes. Miss Cunningham had life insurance, and as a matter of course, her insurance company wants me to look into her death."

He took the business card from her as if it were contaminated with germs. "I will see if Mr. Cunningham will receive you." He closed the door in her face.

Colleen took the opportunity to look around. It was beautiful in this part of Virginia — the grand estates filled with huge deciduous trees that blazed with the glory that only an Eastern autumn could bestow. The brilliant reds, golds, and oranges of the trees were complemented by symmetrical rows of burgundy, yellow, and rust-colored chrysanthemums. The immaculate lawn spread out before her like a velvet cloak in a shade of blue-green that only nature could produce. The stately maples and oaks were placed just perfectly throughout the property, and a couple were even taller than the mansion. Strategically planted bushes surrounded the house like an emerald necklace, but close inspection showed them to be azaleas. In the spring, they would create such a riot of vivid color that she almost wished she'd be here to see it.

Not seeing any cars but her own, she assumed there must be a garage nearby. The house itself was old; Colleen estimated at least 100 years. It was well taken care of and appeared to have been recently painted. Just as she was tempted to step off the porch, the door opened abruptly. The butler looked as if he'd swallowed a bug.

"Mr. Cunningham will see you in the library."

Feeling like she should be wearing a muslin gown out of a Jane Austen novel, Colleen followed his disapproving back down the long hallway carpeted with colorful Oriental rugs. She couldn't help but notice the expensive artwork everywhere — marble and bronze statues of unintelligible shapes, bold contemporary paintings, old tapestries. It seemed a haphazard collection with no common theme.

The butler waved her through a pair of heavy doors. "Miss Fitzgerald, sir."

Colleen stepped past him. The room was dark, its walls covered with mahogany bookshelves stuffed with leather-bound books of every shape and size. The one window was covered with heavy brocade draperies of gold and dark blue. Behind an enormous wooden desk sat Roger Cunningham. His expression wasn't much better than the butler's. He stood as Colleen approached.

They shook hands over the desk, appraising each other. She hoped what he saw was a professional woman dressed in a conservative navy blue suit and white blouse. She saw a man who looked like a gray-haired version of a young Raymond Burr as Perry Mason. He wore a dark blue polo shirt with the requisite designer logo. He was very tall and slender of build. His handshake was firm and warm. He had been writing in what appeared to be a ledger of some kind.

"Mr. Cunningham, may I first say how sorry I am for your loss."

He gestured to a chair. "Thank you. What's this insurance claim? I didn't know Sheila had insurance."

Colleen fidgeted a bit. "Actually, her film company took out the insurance. I'm just checking to make sure there are no loose ends."

"That disgusting company. Starlight? Is that their name? I'm going to sue them, you know. I think they used coercion. Contracts be damned, my Sheila would not do such a thing on her own. I didn't bring her up that way."

"When was the last time you saw your daughter alive, Mr. Cunningham?"

He got up from his chair and came around the desk so he could pace the room. "It's been a few years, I'm ashamed to admit. We didn't exactly get along. She was a great disappointment to me."

"How can you be so sure she wouldn't turn to such a life, then? Perhaps she was desperate for cash?"

"I can't believe she would stoop to such a thing instead of coming to me. I am her father, despite our differences. I loved her."

"So she did need money?"

Cunningham seemed to deflate right before Colleen's eyes. Suddenly he didn't seem quite so tall. The pain in his voice and his eyes affected her. She had to fight the urge to take him in her arms and comfort him as she would her own father.

"I cut her off when I found out about the baby. We exchanged angry words. Said things. Nasty things. I'd give anything now to take that all back."

Despite feeling sorry for him, Colleen couldn't help the cynical thoughts that crept into her mind. It was so typical. People wouldn't swallow their pride and make amends when someone was alive, and then were stuck with the guilt of it for the rest of their lives. She felt it was inexcusable for a parent to do that to a child, even if Sheila's rebelliousness was at least partly to blame.

"That baby was born over eight years ago. You've had no contact with her since then?"

He stopped pacing and sat down again behind the desk. Colleen noted that he didn't contradict her about the baby's birth. "You think I'm terrible, don't you?"

Keeping her true thoughts to herself, she repeated, "Did you have any contact with her?"

"What exactly are you doing here again?"

"Just routine procedure. The insurance company always investigates claims."

"What's that got to do with me?"

Was it her imagination, or did Cunningham seem a little nervous? She watched as he snapped a rubber band back and forth between his two hands. "Nothing really. I just wanted to know if you'd spoken to Sheila. Maybe had an idea of her outlook. It's possible she committed suicide."

The rubber band shot across the room, barely missing her shoulder. His self-control snapped as his fist slammed against the desk. "I'll never believe that! Never!"

Nervous herself now, Colleen soothed, "I didn't

mean to upset you, but you don't know what Sheila's state of mind might have been. You said yourself you hadn't seen or heard from her in years."

"I still can't believe she'd kill herself. She had more pride."

"What kind of pride would allow a young woman to turn to pornography as a profession? She could have been a prostitute for all you know." Or care, she added silently.

He turned blazing eyes on her. His whole body tensed, like a predator ready to spring. "I only just buried her yesterday and you come to me with these kinds of questions? I want you to leave. Now!"

Colleen stood. This interview was most definitely over, but she'd be back. "I'm sorry to have bothered you at this time. I can see myself out."

She left the library and walked down the long hallway, glancing behind her to see if Cunningham followed. The snooty butler was nowhere to be seen. She was surprised. Somehow she thought he'd have been listening at the door, to protect his "master" more than anything else.

She took a deep breath when she walked into the sunshine. The atmosphere in the house was too dismal and somewhat scary. She felt as if she'd been locked away for a long time. There was clearly more to the story than Roger Cunningham was willing to reveal. She found it hard to believe he'd had absolutely no contact with Sheila in all these years. And the grandchild was a product of rape, according to Gillian. What father would disown his own daughter after such a violent act? Assuming he'd known about it, that is. She cursed under her breath for not having asked him. And what had happened to the baby? She assumed Sheila must have given it up for adoption. Or perhaps it had been stillborn.

As Colleen approached her car, she was startled by a short elderly woman who appeared to have been waiting for her. "He tell you about his fight with Sheila?" she asked in a voice hoarse from smoking.

Colleen looked at her. "And who are you?"

The woman motioned her inside the car. "Let's go for a drive, shall we? Don't want to be seen. Hurry."

They both got into the car, and Colleen drove in silence. They were almost to the beltway exit when the woman pointed for her to turn left. They entered a small park. No one else was around.

Colleen turned off the ignition and waited. She was dying of curiosity, but she didn't dare speak. The woman seemed a trifle eccentric. One wrong move or word could scare her away.

"I've worked for the Cunninghams all my life," she began, "and I never liked what Mr. Cunningham did to Sheila. She was such a sweet girl. All she ever wanted was for her daddy to love her. Everything she did was only to get his attention. Even the pornography stuff. Guess she hoped he'd rescue her, but he never did. Bastard!"

Colleen was surprised at her vehemence, but the woman's story, if true, revealed that Cunningham was lying when he claimed he hadn't had contact with Sheila. "Why do you still work for him?"

"I don't stay 'cause of him. I stay in the memory of his dear wife. She died more than six years ago. God rest her soul. Someone has to take care of her things."

"So, you're the housekeeper?"

"No, I'm not in charge of running the house, but

I have my own duties. I can't let him get away with what he did."

"And what is that?"

The woman looked at her, her dark blue eyes flashing. "He tortured her. Told her she could come home, then when she'd show up, he'd tell her he'd changed his mind. Told her to go back to doing those unspeakable things."

Colleen was shocked. Her first impression of Roger Cunningham had been that he was cold, but that he could be so sadistic . . . "What do you know about Sheila's baby?"

"That was so long ago." She looked out the window for a while before speaking again. "I remember hearing him on the phone one night. I think she had a boy 'cause Mr. Cunningham told her the child would never bear his name. The whole situation 'bout near drove Mrs. Cunningham to her death, but she lived two more years. Cancer, poor thing. Never spoke again to her only child. He wouldn't let her."

"He controlled his wife that much?"

"Runs that house with an iron fist, he does. She was afraid of him. They both were. I know he hit them sometimes, but they never complained."

"Sheila didn't come home when her mother got sick? Or for the funeral?"

The woman sighed. "We didn't know where she was. I called everyone I could think of — all her friends. None had heard from her."

"When was the last time you know for sure that Mr. Cunningham talked to Sheila. Please think. This is very important."

Just then a car drove into the parking lot. The

woman looked around and nervously pulled her flimsy sweater tighter. "I've got to get back." She hesitated. "He talked to her a few days before she died. She called to tell him she was in town and could she see him. He told her he'd see her dead first."

Colleen started the car. "Listen, I need to talk to you again. Maybe you could meet with me later, at the mall perhaps?"

"I've said all I'm gonna say. Just take me home. And don't call me. I'll deny I ever spoke to you."

After Colleen dropped the woman off, one block from the house at her request, she realized she hadn't asked her name. But the information she'd gotten was very interesting, and she wondered how she could use it to her advantage. She decided to call Bob Jones again. With his personal interest in Sheila, he might know who called her and if any calls came from her father. And a father who said he'd rather see his daughter dead most certainly belonged on her suspect list.

Chapter Seven

Colleen managed to find a parking space close to home. As she approached her building, she couldn't help but smile. The late afternoon sun cast a warm glow across its red brick exterior. The two trees that graced its entrance rivaled the red with their own autumn glow. As always, Colleen felt lucky that she'd found the cute little apartment not far from DuPont Circle. And the anticipation that Gillian probably waited for her inside brought a spring to her step. She practically sprinted up the stairs.

"Honey, I'm home," she called out as she opened the door. It felt so good to say.

Gillian came out of the bathroom, her dark hair damp from the shower. She vigorously rubbed it with a towel. Her white T-shirt was short enough to reveal white bikini underwear. Both contrasted wonderfully with her dark brown skin. The tall, muscular body always took Colleen's breath away.

Gillian kissed Colleen's cheek. She smelled like soap and talcum powder. Colleen grabbed Gillian's head and kissed her mouth. "I've missed you."

Gillian smiled. "I missed you too. Where the hell have you been anyway? I called your office several times."

Colleen took a deep breath. "Actually, I went to see Roger Cunningham."

Just as Colleen anticipated, Gillian was indignant. "You went without me?"

"I thought it best. Besides, you said yourself it wouldn't be good for you to be seen. I found out some interesting information though."

"Oh?"

Colleen led Gillian over to the couch. "For one thing," she said as they sat down, "Sheila did have the baby, a boy. But I don't know what happened to him."

A look of sadness crossed Gillian's face. "I'm not surprised she had the baby. Roger told you?"

"Not really. It was a strange little woman who works in the house. She accosted me as I was leaving and had me drive to a secluded park. There's no love lost between her and Sheila's father."

Gillian gave a short laugh. "That had to be Mercy

Warner. She's been with the family since Sheila was a baby. She sort of acted like a nanny, but then I'm not sure what her role became. She loved Mrs. Cunningham and Sheila, but disliked Roger intensely. At least, that's what Sheila told me."

"She accused him of beating them."

"Hmmm, I never saw any evidence of it. Of course, we were in college, but she never mentioned it. What else did you learn?"

"That Cunningham is lying when he claims he's had no contact with Sheila all these years. She'd call and he'd tell her to come home, and then when she arrived, he'd say he'd changed his mind."

Gillian's green eyes darkened with anger.

"That's not the best part. According to Mercy, he talked to Sheila a few days before she died. She wanted to see him, but he said he'd see her dead first."

Gillian looked incredulous. "You think he could have killed her? His own daughter?"

Colleen threw up her hands. "I don't really see how. I mean, she *was* an addict. And a man like that would most definitely have been noticed."

"Yeah, you're right." Gillian pushed Colleen down on the couch. "But, enough of this talk." She kissed Colleen's neck. "I just want to show you how happy I am to be with you."

Colleen put her arms around Gillian's strong shoulders. "Mmmm, you'll have no argument from me."

* * * * *

70

As usual, the weekend had passed too quickly. Colleen had talked Gillian into going to Skyline Drive in Virginia to enjoy the fall foliage in its most vibrant colors. They'd found a little bed and breakfast to stay in Saturday night, and had spent Sunday exploring the Luray and Skyline caverns. It was one of those things Colleen always meant to do, but never did.

In the office Monday morning, Colleen tried to reach Bob Jones. A female voice told her he no longer worked for Starlight Studios. Colleen was sure that somehow Jackson Ramses had found out about her interview with Jones and had sacked him. The voice refused to give Colleen any more information. As she hung up, she wondered if there was any way to track him down. Surely he must belong to some theatrical trade union? She knew no one in the movie industry, but she made a note on her list of things to do. This was not a good turn of events. She wanted to talk to him again about Rick Ewing, the fan, and she was sure he'd know about the born-again protester, Randy Wilson, too.

Not having heard from Jenna Bolden, Colleen tried her home phone number. When she got Jenna's answering machine, she couldn't help the shiver that crept up her spine when she heard the low-throated voice. There was just something about a husky-voiced butch . . .

After leaving a message, Colleen looked at her list of possible suspects. It seemed like her best bet was to go back to the studio and see who was hanging around. Amber's obsessed fan would probably be putting up some kind of memorial, and the ex-porn star might be giving some kind of I-told-you-so speech. At least, she hoped they would be. She wondered if Gillian would want to go with her, but when she called the apartment, no one answered.

Taking a taxi this time, Colleen arrived at the studio in Southeast a little before eleven. Promising the cab driver a $10 tip if he'd wait for her, she walked over to the trailers. Sure enough, flowers adorned the steps leading to Amber's. A glass jar nestled among the blooms, but remembering Bob Jones' comments, she didn't examine it too closely.

"Get the hell away from there!"

Colleen jumped at the loud voice and turned toward its owner, remaining on the step. A man walked rapidly from the left corner of the trailer. He wasn't very tall — maybe five-six, with a slim build. His curly black hair was thinning in the front. As he got closer, she could see his heavily pock-marked face. His angry expression made her nervous.

"My name is Colleen Fitzgerald. I'm an insurance investigator."

He came to a stop and stood looking up at her, his hands on his hips in a gesture of displeasure and his chest puffed out like a fighting rooster. "I didn't ask your name. I told you to go away."

"Do you work for the studio?"

"No. I don't. But if I did, Amber would still be alive today."

"I'm sorry. I didn't get your name."

"I didn't give it to you."

Colleen thought she might have more success with him if she came down off the step, but she was a little afraid. She was sure this must be Rick Ewing. As she considered what to do, he seemed to deflate. His hands dropped to his sides and he lowered his eyes. He was all show.

"You must have liked Amber very much," Colleen said, hoping her tone was sufficiently sympathetic. "These flowers are from you?"

"Yes, I loved her. I wanted to take her away from all this, but that bastard wouldn't let her go."

"You mean Mr. Ramses?"

"Yes."

"How well did you know Amber? Did you know about her drug habit?"

"Do you have to stay up there? It hurts my neck to look at you."

Colleen came down the steps. She was the taller of the two, which made her feel more secure. It was awkward standing in the warehouse parking lot, but this part of town didn't exactly boast many restaurants or cafés where they could sit down with a cup of coffee. There was only one thing to do — take him to her waiting taxi and return to the office.

"Will you come with me to my office? I have a taxi right over there."

"Well, I suppose it couldn't hurt."

They walked to the cab together, but didn't speak another word until they got to her office. She settled him in front of her desk.

"Can I get you something to drink?"

"No, thanks."

She pulled out her notepad. "Do you think you could give me your name now?"

"Yeah. Rick Ewing."

"And where do you live, Mr. Ewing?"

"Here and there. I follow Amber wherever she's filming."

"How long have you done that?"

"About four years now. I tried so hard to show how much I loved her, but she wouldn't listen. That damn producer always had me thrown off the property. It was easy to get in here though, no private lot."

"I understand you had a restraining order?"

He laughed. The sound grated on her nerves. "No one cares about those things."

"What do you know about her drug habit?"

"I know who was supplying her. It was that creep, Hobie somebody. He kept all the actors supplied. Made manipulating them much easier."

"Why do you think she overdosed this time?"

He shrugged. "It was just her time. She'd suffered enough. If I could have taken her away, it wouldn't have happened. She's better off now, I suppose."

"Do you think someone helped her?"

His attitude changed. "What do you want with me?" he asked testily.

Colleen decided to switch tactics. "Information. That's all. Do you work, Mr. Ewing?"

He shook his head. "I'll take odd jobs here and there, but I'm on disability." He grinned. "The checks just follow me around."

"I'd like to read you some names now, and you tell me if you saw them at the studio the day Amber died."

He recognized all the names on her suspect list except Roger Cunningham's. Colleen wondered if a man like him would even go to such a place. It was unlikely, but she described him to Rick anyway. He hadn't seen anyone matching Roger's description, but he mentioned that he'd seen men among the anti-porn protesters at times.

"You've been a great help, Mr. Ewing. Just one more thing. Where were you that day around the time Amber died?"

He surprised Colleen by not getting angry. "I already told the police. I was at the pharmacy getting a prescription filled. I had to wait over an hour. When I got back to the lot, the police had already cordoned off the trailer." He took a deep breath that sounded like a sob. "I had to watch them take away her dear, sweet body in that impersonal rubber bag."

"What medication are you taking?"

A spark of anger flared up this time. "Not that it's any of your business, but I take Paxil. It's for depression." He stood abruptly. "I have to go now."

Colleen stood too. She held out her card, which he ignored. "Thanks for talking to me. I'm sure I'll call on you again."

He marched out of her office and was down the hall before she could come from around her desk to escort him out. By the time she got to her door, she saw him disappear around the corner. Lisa Anderson approached from the opposite direction, hands on hips as if glued there.

"Who was that queer little man?" she asked as she sauntered into Colleen's office.

"One of the people I'm talking to about the Starlight case. He liked to leave the dead woman presents of his sperm."

Lisa stuck out her tongue. "That is so gross. You really get some strange cases."

Colleen laughed. "What cases? This is only my second one. My career as an investigator will be a short one if they're all this intense."

Lisa sat in the chair vacated by Rick and crossed her impossibly long legs. The miniskirt was absent today, replaced by blue leggings topped with a matching blue sweater. Colleen wished her new boss wasn't quite so attractive.

"Why don't you bring me up to date on the case?"

Lisa made the question sound like an invitation to take a shower together. Colleen took a deep breath and complied.

Chapter Eight

A little past seven that evening, Colleen and Gillian were waiting at La Tomate Restaurant on Connecticut Avenue. Jenna Bolden had finally returned Colleen's call and could only get together for dinner. Colleen suspected Jenna's intentions, and decided to bring Gillian along to dispel any notions Jenna might have as far as Colleen's availability.

Gillian's back was to the entrance, but she must have seen something in Colleen's eyes because she turned around rather quickly. Jenna strode confidently to the table. She looked positively

stunning in a dark, man-tailored suit cut to
pin-striped perfection. She wore a red tie with the
pristine white Oxford shirt. Diamond links glittered
in the cuffs. Her leather briefcase was obviously
expensive and matched her equally expensive shoes.
Remembering the jean-clad Jenna she'd met at Food
for Thought, Colleen was speechless and totally
oblivious to Gillian's scowl.

"So sorry I'm late," Jenna said as she sat down.
"I was tied up in court."

"No problem," Colleen managed to say. "This is
my friend, Gillian Smith. Gillian, Jenna Bolden."

"Hello."

Colleen looked at Gillian. Something in her tone
didn't sound quite right, and she did not look happy.
"Are you okay, Gillian?"

"Of course."

She placed her hand casually over Colleen's and
smiled at Jenna, but Colleen thought it looked more
like a grimace. She glanced over at Jenna, who was
smiling too. The two of them looked like fighters
sizing each other up in the ring. Colleen felt
possession in the way Gillian held her hand, almost
too firmly. She tried to ease her hand away, but
Gillian held fast.

"Well, shall we talk business first and then order
dinner?" Colleen asked.

"Sure," Jenna said, her voice sending ripples of
pleasure through Colleen's body. "I expect this is
about Amber Rose. You've found out that my group
regularly protests Starlight, and that I was there the
day she died."

"Why didn't you tell me before?" Colleen asked.

Jenna laughed. "I didn't want to spoil our evening out. Brian had gone to so much trouble to introduce us."

As Gillian's grip on her hand tightened, Colleen glanced at her in surprise. Gillian was not bothering to hide her displeasure now. Colleen smiled to herself. So, her lover was actually jealous.

"I don't suppose you have any members who might think a dead porn star is better than a live one?"

Now it was Jenna's turn frown. "We're against violence against women."

"Oh, and those pro-lifers who murder abortion doctors and bomb clinics are perfect examples of what being pro-life means," Gillian retorted.

Jenna looked at her and raised an eyebrow. "I assume you're trying to make the point that someone opposed to violence isn't necessarily incapable of committing such an act? Well, this is a little different from those who think killing someone will stop the killing of others. None in my group would have injected Amber with a lethal drug. We want these women to leave that way of life, not sacrifice their own."

"Well, I don't see how making movies can be construed as violence," Gillian argued.

"Pornography, to us, is a form of violence. A lot of those women are forced into the life against their will. They are raped and abused constantly. And in my line of work, I have seen evidence that men who watch porn can become violent themselves."

Colleen didn't like the way the conversation was going. She was beginning to regret having brought Gillian. There was more going on here than just jealousy. She managed to withdraw her hand and give Gillian a reassuring pat. "Amber was once a close friend of Gillian's."

"I'm very sorry," Jenna said. "I can only tell you that when Amber died, we had all left for the day. It was a very small group. We all got on the Metro together; no one was left behind."

"Do you mind if I ask you a personal question? Your involvement with this group is not a conflict of interest with your law firm? They don't care if you take time off to protest?"

"It's not something I do on a regular basis. I just happened to be on vacation that week. Starlight is not someone we want to stay in our city." She took a sip of wine. "As to the conflict of interest . . . Well, I'm in family law, not criminal law. And as long as it doesn't interfere with my work, the partners don't care about what I do in my free time."

Colleen nodded, not fully convinced. "And you saw nothing out of the ordinary that day? Someone hanging around the trailer? A fight in the parking lot?"

"No, nothing. We merely handed out literature as the actors and crew arrived and then left. We had our signs, but we weren't loud."

"Any men with you that day?"

"No."

"You won't mind if I talk to the others?"

"Not at all." Jenna reached into her briefcase. "Here's a list of names. I anticipated your request."

She tapped the paper and gave Colleen a suggestive grin. "My address is on there too."

"You must be an awfully good lawyer," Gillian commented, her tone belying her words.

"I think we should order dinner now," Colleen said and quickly opened her menu.

Colleen and Gillian walked home from the restaurant in silence. The balmy October night went unappreciated. Colleen usually loved to walk along Connecticut Avenue in the evening. She would stroll casually, looking in all the store windows, perhaps stopping at Lambda Rising to say hello to Brian or at the Circle Bar for her standard 7UP with lime. She would smile at all the gay people, real or perceived. This night, however, she walked rapidly, her thoughts churning along with her anger. Gillian's continued sullen attitude during the entire dinner had left Colleen with a bad taste in her mouth. Jenna had remained cheerful, doing most of the talking for all three of them. She had held Colleen's hand just a tad too long in her farewell handshake, and her eyes had held Colleen's in a bold yet unspoken invitation.

Colleen barely noticed the colorful mums that lined the streets or the last vestiges of autumn glory that shone under the street lamps. Once inside the building, she clattered up the stairs, unmindful of Gillian trailing behind. She ignored the gray cat that met her at the door and rubbed against her legs. Instead, she turned as Gillian came through the door.

"You were positively monstrous tonight!"

"I don't like that woman," Gillian retorted.

"That's no excuse for being rude. She is part of my investigation. I didn't appreciate your attitude."

"And I didn't appreciate your flirting with her right in front of me."

"Flirting? I was not flirting. Don't tell me you're one of those women who's jealous when her girlfriend talks to another woman."

"Why don't you just be honest with yourself. You're attracted to her. And why is Brian setting you up with other women anyway?"

Colleen took off her coat and threw it on the couch. "Maybe it's because my lover refuses to leave the beach. When was the last time we saw each other? And why do I always have to be the one who comes to you?"

"I'm here now."

Colleen laughed, the sound harsh, even to her own ears. "You're only here because of Sheila. I think you're hiding something."

"I don't believe it. You think I had something to do with the death of a woman I haven't seen in years? Like you thought I had with Candy's?"

"Don't be absurd. I know you had nothing to do with Sheila's death, but you haven't been entirely honest with me. I always have to find out things in a roundabout way."

"Like you have no secrets."

"Well, I don't. My life is pretty boring next to your jetset ways. And we're not talking about me."

In answer, Gillian came over and took Colleen's stiff body in her arms. She kissed Colleen's neck, then stroked Colleen's shoulders and arms. Colleen felt her anger draining away, no matter how hard she tried to keep it. Her own hands seemed to circle Gillian's neck on their own volition. She responded to Gillian's kisses as they became more insistent. It wasn't long before she lay naked under Gillian's strong body, feeling only Gillian's mouth and fingers as they drove all thoughts of Jenna from her mind.

The next morning, Colleen decided it was time to pay another visit to Roger Cunningham. She had lots of questions for him, especially about his claim that he hadn't had contact with his daughter. She was also surprised that no one from the film studio had called her. She was sure she would have heard from at least one. It was time to track them down individually and talk to them without Jackson Ramses present. She was convinced he knew more about Sheila's death than he was letting on, and if he was involved in any way, it would invalidate his insurance claim.

"What are your plans for today?" she asked Gillian as they drank their morning coffee and ate fresh apple turnovers. Gillian had risen early and gone to the bakery around the corner.

"I'd like to corrupt you into taking the day off."

"Unfortunately, I have a lot of work to do. I'm going to talk to Cunningham again, and the people at the film studio."

"I think I should go with you. I don't like the idea of your having to deal with those people."

Colleen smiled. She liked Gillian's protectiveness.

"You could come with me, but I think you'd be bored. Also, Roger might not talk to me if you're there."

"Well, I've got friends over in Arlington. Guess I can go look them up." She stood and stretched.

Two kisses later, Colleen was on her way back to McLean. Rush-hour traffic going out of the city wasn't bad, but once on the beltway it was horrendous. She was not in a good mood as she entered the Cunningham estate. Before she could even get out of the car, the butler was on his way down the steps.

"Mr. Cunningham is not seeing anyone now," he said as she opened the car door.

"How nice of you to come out and meet me. Please tell Mr. Cunningham I won't take up much of his time. And that I am not leaving until he sees me."

"I will call the police and have you removed."

She leaned back against the hood of the car and folded her arms. "Then call them."

They stood and stared at each other. He glared down at her from his height of over six feet. He looked away first and went into the house without another word.

To her surprise, Roger came out himself. He did not invite her in, but leaned against her car too, with his arms casually crossed. The lack of formality unnerved her a bit. He gave her a sad smile.

"Miss Fitzgerald, I don't know what you think you might discover by coming out here. I loved my daughter."

She couldn't help herself. "If you loved her, why were you so cruel? Why did you invite her home and then reject her time and time again?"

He gave a bitter laugh. "Oh, I see you've been talking to Mercy Warner. She never did approve of me. I didn't do that to Sheila to be cruel. I hoped that one day she would tell me she was through with that life. I guess I used the carrot-on-a-stick routine. Dangling the good life in front of her so she'd know what she was missing. Believe me, it was like stabbing myself over and over again each time she left."

"Why did Sheila hate you so much?"

He uncrossed his arms and began pacing alongside the car. "When Sheila was twelve, she found out I'd been cheating on her mother. The irony is, her mother never found out, but Sheila never forgave me. From that point on, our lives were a constant battle." He laughed again, harshly. "The whole pornography thing . . . It was her final insult to everything I stood for. Nothing else had worked to shame me. Not her homosexual lifestyle, not the illegitimate birth."

Colleen pushed away from the car. That wasn't what Gillian had theorized. "You knew she was gay and it didn't bother you?"

"Of course. I knew everything about her, and none of it mattered." He stopped and gazed at Colleen, the deep pain evident in his expression. If it wasn't real, he was an awfully good actor. The look in his eyes changed to one of nostalgic adoration. "She was so exquisite, her skin so soft and white, her hair like silken golden threads. That magnificent body. When she smiled at me, I would do anything for her. I loved her more than anyone else in the world."

The way he spoke triggered a horrible suspicion. Before she could hold her tongue, she blurted out, "Were you intimate with your daughter?"

Fury replaced adoration. She instinctively stepped back as he raised his hands. "How *dare* you imply such a thing?" he raged. "If you *ever* make such insinuations again, it will cost you your job. And don't think I can't do it."

Her whole body trembling, Colleen crept around the car to the driver's side. Feeling safer with the automobile between them, she tried to salvage the situation. "I'm so sorry, Mr. Cunningham. I don't know what I was thinking. It was very unprofessional of me."

He appeared to calm down, but tension still rippled across his broad shoulders. "I don't understand what all this has to do with Sheila's death. You're supposed to be investigating the legitimacy of Starlight's claim. I have nothing to do with that."

"I'm aware that you knew when Sheila arrived in the city. Why did you tell her you'd 'see her dead first' when she called?"

He laughed, the sound sending chills up Colleen's spine. "I never did like Mercy. That nosy busybody is more trouble than she's worth. You've heard the phrase, 'a figure of speech'?"

This time Colleen laughed. "You want me to believe a perceived death threat to your own daughter was merely a figure of speech?"

He clenched his jaw. "You don't understand me or

my daughter. Go on and chase your fantasies elsewhere. If I see you here again, I'll have you charged with trespassing."

Colleen opened her car door. "I'm sorry to have bothered you. I apologize for any impertinence."

Without another word, Cunningham turned on his heel. By the time he'd gotten to the door, Colleen was backing out of the driveway as fast as possible. The last time she'd seen anger like his was when Albert Simmons had kidnapped her on her last case. The fearful memory made the adrenaline surge through her body. She didn't care how much Roger claimed to love Sheila. Rage like that made people do crazy things. She didn't dismiss for a moment that he could have killed his own daughter. He did have one point, she had to admit. It was Starlight Studios she should be concentrating her efforts on.

As Colleen exited onto the Capital Beltway, she decided to head into Southeast Washington and visit the studio again. She would insist on speaking to everyone individually and in private, even if it meant delaying production.

Chapter Nine

Colleen had no trouble locating the warehouse again. Under the cloudy sky, it seemed even more grim than before. She parked the car and walked toward a small group of protesters gathered outside Sheila's trailer. They carried hand-written signs. Jenna was not among them, and she felt a little pang of disappointment. Standing away from the others, but watching curiously, were two homeless men.

A wild-haired man with blazing black eyes pointed animatedly at the trailer. His strident voice penetrated the air, sending goosebumps up Colleen's arms. " 'Dogs of the stree't," he shrilled, " 'shall eat the flesh of Jezebel, and the corpse of Jezebel shall be refuse on the surface of the field.' "

Colleen was taken aback. He didn't seem to fit the kind of image Jenna had portrayed of her group. Then she noticed that the people standing around him looked uncomfortable. They whispered among themselves, not really paying attention to his ravings.

"You must all repent," the wild man continued. "Let Jesus into your hearts so you may recognize the evil that is Starlight and everyone like them. For it is written, 'To the carnally minded is death, but to the spiritually minded is life and peace'!"

"What's going on here?" Colleen asked the woman closest to her.

"It's just Ravin' Randy again. He seems to show up every time we come. He doesn't realize we're here for the same thing — to put an end to the wickedness that is pornography. He has some really bizarre ideas though."

"Bizarre?"

"Yeah. Used to be in the business himself. One of their biggest stars. Ever hear of Randy Rodman?" Colleen looked at her blankly. "Well anyway, he contracted HIV and now blames the porn industry, especially Starlight 'cause he shot most of his videos with them. He became born again, but he preaches death and destruction. He was even arrested one time for possessing a gun."

"You're with Jenna Bolden's group?"

The woman appraised her. "The group to which she also belongs, do you mean?"

"Well, yes."

"And what's your interest in all this? You a reporter or something?"

"I'm an insurance investigator to see Jackson Ramses. Tell me, were you here when Amber Rose died?"

"Not that day. I was sick."

Colleen gestured to the crowd. "How about any of the others?"

"You'll have to ask them."

"I will. Excuse me, please."

As she headed to the warehouse entrance, the group around Randy Wilson began to break up. She caught a glimpse of Rick Ewing as he laid an object on the steps to the trailer. It seemed as if all the weirdos had come out together. Politically touchy though it was, Colleen had always thought the anti-porn feminists a little too ardent. And here they were, together with a born-again ex-porn star and an obsessed fan. Strong beliefs sure could make strange bedfellows, Colleen mused as she opened the heavy door and stepped into the warehouse.

She followed the dim corridor along the same path she'd taken before. She could hear voices up ahead. When it seemed she had the right door, she flung it open and was greeted with a tirade of colorful language. Jackson Ramses came striding over.

"Who the hell do you think you are? We're right in the middle of a shoot!"

Colleen found herself apologizing for the second time that day. She couldn't help but glance toward the center of the room. It appeared to be a retake of what she'd seen the first time she visited the set.

She wondered why they didn't tape the scene once and just keep replaying it.

"I really need to talk to your people again, but this time I want to borrow your office and talk to them individually."

"You should have called and made the arrangements. I can't just quit now. Amber's replacement is finally ready and we've got to make up for lost time."

That's when Colleen noticed the new girl. And she was nothing but a girl. If she was eighteen, Colleen would get up on that big bed herself. She was a younger version of Sheila. The resemblance was so strong it was scary. She was very blonde and very pretty and looked very scared.

"How old is that girl?" she hissed so no one but Jackson could hear.

"She's nineteen, and it's none of your business. Now, could we do this later?"

"No. And if you give me trouble, I will do a little investigating on my own into your new star's background."

Jackson scowled at her before turning and clapping his hands. "Okay everyone, we're taking a little break. Miss Fitzgerald here would like to finish up with each of you privately."

One of the male stars pointed to his semi-erect penis and said, "Is Miss Fitzgerald gonna finish this too?"

Mortified, Colleen felt her face flush furiously as they all snickered. All but the girl, that is, who lowered her eyes and blushed too. Jackson pointed to the redhead. "Julia, you go first."

She followed Jackson and Colleen to the little office. He glared at Colleen once more before he left them alone. Colleen motioned for Julia to sit.

"There's no reason to be nervous," Colleen began.

"I'm not nervous at all." Julia's throaty voice oozed over Colleen like honey. She crossed incredibly long legs, letting her filmy baby-blue negligee glide up her thigh. "You just tell me what you need, and I'll give it to you."

Colleen swallowed. Julia's words may not have been meant as an invitation, but they sure sounded like one. "Just tell me what you know about the day Amber died. Maybe a little about the fight she and Jackson had."

"They always fought. It was nothing new. Jackson treats his girls all the same. He can be condescending and cruel. I told Amber to get out if she couldn't handle it."

"Was she causing problems with the production? If she was sick often, did she hold things up?"

"Honey, in this business, you're not allowed to be sick. You're expected to suck and swallow and smile even if you're sick as a dog, which Amber was most of the time. Guess that stuff she shot up her arm wasn't good enough."

"So you all knew about her habit?"

"Sure."

"Are you an addict too, Miss Osborne?"

Julia laughed, tossing her red hair over her shoulder like the pro that she was. "Not anymore. I kicked it. But that's an awfully personal question."

"Did Sheila, I mean Amber, seem depressed that day?"

"Not more than usual. There's this psycho, Rick

something, who says he loves her. He was hanging around that day, and he always riled her up. And then there was ol' Ravin' Randy and his harangues. He got on everyone's nerves, but he made Amber particularly jumpy." She leaned forward conspiratorially, her full breasts catching Colleen's eye. "Maybe it's 'cause they did a few videos together. Maybe she thought she had AIDS too."

"I heard Randy outside today," Colleen said. "Not a very pleasant guy."

Julia shrugged and leaned back. "He has a right to be bitter. I would be too."

"Just who exactly does he blame for his becoming infected with HIV?"

"Oh, everybody. He was gay for pay."

"Gay for pay?"

"Yeah, he did gay videos too, but he wasn't gay himself. Hey, listen, you're a nice girl, but I can't help you with this."

"You seemed a bit nervous the first time I was here. Why is that?"

"God, I really could use a cigarette. Don't suppose you have one?"

Colleen shook her head.

"Look, I was just jumpy that day. I mean, Amber had only died a week or so before. It took us all a while to get back to normal. We really are a family around here." She stood up, towering over Colleen. "I don't have anything more to tell you. Good luck."

"One more question, please. What happened to Bob Jones?"

"Happened? Nothing happened. He just left one day. It's no surprise in this business. Jackson was furious."

Colleen watched her leave, wondering what circumstances had led her to porn. She was beautiful, and with that body and that height, she could easily have been a model. She chided herself once again for succumbing to stereotyping. Beauty did not guarantee success, nor did it protect from the seedier aspects of life.

She smiled as Lance Lawson, the cameraman, entered. He was another one she had thought was nervous on her first visit. This time he was nonchalant, seemingly unaffected by Amber's death. He answered her questions perfunctorily. No, Amber didn't seem more depressed than usual. No, she and Jackson hadn't had a particularly bad fight. Yes, he knew Amber was an addict. No, Randy and Rick weren't more obnoxious than usual. Yes, Bob Jones just up and left one day. In short, he had nothing new to tell her. She got basically the same answers from Judith Weinberg, who performed under the nom de porn of Tiffany Glass.

One by one the others came in, the other cameraman, Andy Jach, and then the two male stars, Douglas Letter and Chris Iverson. They were the exact opposite of each other — one blonde and short, the other dark-haired and tall. Their bodies had that half-pumped-up look, like men who'd only been going to a gym for a few months. They were good-looking in a smarmy sort of way. They also thought they were charming.

No one had anything new to tell. She was sure they'd all gotten their stories straight before her interviews. And only Chris, the one who looked liked Judith's twin brother, admitted to drug use, but he claimed it to be recreational rather than addictive.

Jackson Ramses came last. He wasn't any happier. "Did you get everything you wanted? Can we get back to business now? You cost me a couple of thousand for these two hours, you know."

"I've finished for today, but I will be back. I do have one question for you. Can you tell me what happened to your production assistant, Bob Jones?"

"We just had a little falling out, that's all. I wasn't happy with his work. He tried to tell me how to do my job. This is my show. I do things my way."

"Where can I reach him?"

"How should I know?"

Colleen knew he was lying. "You must have an address of record. You people do run things like any other business, don't you? Filing taxes and such?"

His handsome face crinkled with annoyance. He strode to the file cabinet and yanked open a drawer. After rifling through it for several minutes, he pulled out a plain folder. He scanned down the pages inside, then wrote an address on a piece of paper and flung it on the desk.

"There's his 'address of record'." His tone mocked her. "Now, if you'll excuse me, I have a video to make."

"One more thing. I'd like to talk to your new actress. What's her name?"

"She's got nothing to say. She barely knew Amber."

"Oh? I was under the impression she had just arrived."

He turned and stalked out of the office without answering. This was her day for having angry men turn their backs on her. She scooped up Jones' address and left the room. Production had begun on

95

the video. She couldn't help but pause and watch with both disgust and fascination. Julia was on the bed with the two men. She rested on her hands and knees, her mouth working over Douglas' penis while Chris entered her from behind. Judith was splayed across the pillows at the top of the bed, seeming to watch with pure lust as she masturbated with a huge dildo. Jackson barked orders. The new girl was nowhere to be seen. Lance Lawson caught Colleen staring and gave her a lecherous wink.

Colleen fled the room, feeling slightly nauseated as she navigated the dim corridor. She did not normally consider herself a prude, despite her Catholic upbringing. And she certainly did not believe in censorship of any kind, but she found herself hard-pressed to want to do anything but shut down Jackson's whole operation. She thought about the young girl who was taking Amber's place, and wished she could snatch her up and take her away.

Colleen stumbled into the parking lot, the bright light almost blinding her. She caught her foot and felt herself falling, but someone grabbed her. She was sobbing and didn't even realize it until then. Through her tears she recognized Jenna. She took great gulps of air, trying to stop crying, but the tears wouldn't stop.

"Colleen, what's wrong?" she heard Jenna ask, but she could say nothing. She clung to her until finally she took one deep breath and found herself calm once again. She knew she should pull away from Jenna's arms, but they felt so good around her that she just rested against her strong body. "What's wrong?" Jenna asked again.

Colleen sniffed. "I'm so sorry, Jenna. I don't really

know what happened. One minute I'm being all professional, questioning people, and the next I'm crying like a baby."

"Something must have happened in there."

Colleen reluctantly pulled away. She took a tissue from her purse and blew her nose. "No. It was just so difficult. After I questioned everyone, they didn't wait until I was gone before resuming filming. I had to walk by the set. The things those women were doing...I found it repulsive and degrading."

"Now do you understand why we come here to protest?"

"I never really thought about it. I mean, I saw part of one of these films when I was younger, but I . . . Oh, I don't know. I'm so confused. Why would anyone do this?"

Jenna smiled. "Why don't we have dinner and I'll try to explain it."

"Don't you want to join your friends?"

"I think I'd rather have dinner with a beautiful woman, even one with red eyes and a red nose."

Colleen felt herself blushing. Jenna's grin widened, her brown eyes twinkling with merriment, but Colleen didn't think Jenna was laughing at her. "I think I'd like that." She looked at her watch. "Oh my God, I can't believe it's this late. I'd like to go home and change first."

"And pick up your protector?"

"My protector?"

Jenna grinned again, a little cynical this time. "Your butch little girlfriend. Gillian."

Colleen blushed again. She ran her left hand nervously through her hair. She had a funny feeling in her stomach, but whether from guilt or the little thrill she got from thinking Jenna was jealous, she couldn't tell.

"No, I don't think I'll bring Gillian this time. She just gets bored by business talk. And besides, she's visiting friends in Virginia."

Jenna smiled knowingly. "I understand. Shall we meet at Trumpets?"

"That's a little too expensive for me, I'm afraid."

Jenna took her arm and escorted her to the car without giving her fellow protesters a second look. Only five of them were left standing silently and holding signs. Randy Wilson and Rick Ewing were both gone. Jenna held the door of the raspberry-red Saturn.

"I wouldn't dream of having you pay," she said, her tone implying she would take no argument. "I'll see you around eight."

Chapter Ten

When Colleen finally got home at seven, Gillian, as expected, was not there. She had the usual messages on her answering machine — her mother complaining that she didn't come out to Gaithersburg to visit enough, her sister in Oregon telling her the latest about her niece, the vet reminding her of Smokey's appointment — but nothing from Gillian. It seemed odd, but she didn't have time to dwell on it. She was meeting Jenna in an hour. Truth be told, she was glad that Gillian wasn't home. This way, she didn't have to explain why she was going to dinner without her.

She fed the cat and took a shower, all in record time. Deciding what to wear took a little longer. She chose black, tailored slacks and a royal-blue silk shirt that brought out the blue in her eyes. Throwing on a coat as she raced out the door, she prayed she wouldn't meet Gillian on the way down. She hailed a cab to take her to Trumpets.

Jenna was already waiting. The table was set back in a corner. A most romantic situation if this was a date, Colleen thought as she slid into her seat. Jenna had stood as Colleen approached, and then she kissed her lightly on the cheek and sat down.

"Right on time," she said. "I like that. I took the liberty of ordering wine. Do you drink?"

"No, I'm sorry. Just 7UP with lime, please."

"No problem." Jenna waved the waiter over to cancel the wine and order new drinks. They perused the menu. It had so many exotic entrees to choose from, most of which Colleen could not eat because she was vegetarian. She chose not to mention that fact to Jenna and settled on farfalle pasta with mushrooms and snow peas in a light cream sauce. Jenna ordered the same and then settled back in her chair to study Colleen.

Colleen felt a little uncomfortable under Jenna's scrutiny. "Did I forget to comb my hair?" she asked.

Jenna smiled. "You look wonderful. I was just admiring."

Colleen felt the blood rush to her cheeks. "So, tell me about your group. And why were you there today?"

"I just swung by after a meeting with a client on

Capitol Hill. When I saw your car, I stopped." She lightly touched Colleen's hand before continuing. "First, let me tell you that being anti-porn does not mean we are anti-sex. From a feminist perspective, we believe pornography helps maintain the sexual subordination and oppression of women."

"The actresses I've spoken with don't seem to object to what they're doing. Although, today I did see one who seemed awfully young. Jackson Ramses claims she's nineteen, but I doubt it."

"Don't be fooled by their attitudes. I find it hard to believe that anyone would do videos like that because they really enjoyed it. They might convince themselves they like it, but sooner or later they realize the truth. And some have been coerced."

"How can you be so sure? I mean, I don't want to think they actually like it either, but people are different. What's right for someone else isn't necessarily right for me. Or you. And we don't know their financial situations."

"In my line of work, I've seen how violence and incest can affect families. I see a correlation between hardcore pornography and these things. And yes, I realize poverty, or the threat of it, can drive people to make difficult choices."

"So your group protests in the hopes that you might change someone's mind? Show them other choices?"

Jenna leaned back in her chair again. Colleen had to admit she looked awfully good in the gray tweed jacket that emphasized her broad shoulders. And the dark hair and brown eyes were exactly what she liked in a woman. She couldn't help wondering what it would feel like to be pulled into those strong arms and kissed with that sensual mouth. She looked away as waves of guilt washed over her. She felt as if she were cheating on Gillian.

"Well, that's always the hope. But we're also trying to get the media to pick up on the story to get a dialog going on this — and give the film company some bad publicity."

"Amber's death certainly generated a lot of publicity. Could someone in your group have . . ."

"I can't predict what people will or won't do, but that group is made of pretty staid professional women and a few men. You've got the list if you want to check them out."

Colleen didn't say anything as the waiter brought their food and refills on the drinks. Then she said, "This porn stuff is so confusing."

"I'd be glad to recommend some books for you to read. There's always Andrea Dworkin's works, of course, but a new book just out is Gail Dines' *Pornography: The Production and Consumption of Inequality.* Another good one is John Stoltenberg's *Refusing to Be a Man.*"

Colleen held up her hand and laughed. "Whoa! One at a time, please."

As they ate, the conversation turned to other things. Colleen found herself telling Jenna all about her childhood, how she got into investigating, and how she met Gillian. Jenna was genuinely horrified by the ordeal Colleen went through on her last case. Reliving the nightmare of her kidnapping by Albert Simmons made her think of the people she had met in Rehoboth. People she hadn't spoken to for weeks. She told Jenna about Stephan and Phillip and how Phillip seemed to have beaten the odds with his illness, at least for now. And of course there were Bianca and Suzanne and Vera. Talking about them made her homesick for the beach.

"But enough about myself," Colleen said. "Tell me about Jenna Bolden."

"I'm afraid I don't have as exciting a story to tell as you. I was born in New York, but grew up in Vermont. My mother and younger brother died in a car accident when I was twelve, and I was raised mostly by her sister. My father didn't have time for me after the accident, but I followed his footsteps into law. While he chose corporate law, I went into family law."

Colleen sipped an after-dinner espresso. "Do you and your dad have a good relationship?"

Jenna laughed with a touch of bitterness. "Not after he found out I prefer women. He had it all planned out. I would marry his partner's son and we'd be one big happy family. He was disappointed in my choice of specialty *and* my choice of romantic partner."

Colleen couldn't help thinking that Jenna was the second woman she'd met whose father had freaked out, as had Sheila's. "That's what makes me afraid to tell my folks. I think I've only met one person whose family didn't go ballistic."

"Well, I haven't spoken to my father in five years and that suits me just fine."

"And what about women? Do you have a girlfriend?" Colleen felt herself tensing as she waited for Jenna's answer.

"Not at the moment. I was in a relationship for about four years, but she felt I was spending too much time at the office. I've been single over a year now." She took Colleen's hand. "And what about you and Gillian? How serious is it?"

Colleen felt Jenna's touch like an electric current. It traveled from her fingertips up her arm and spread across her body. Her lips tingled as if they'd been kissed. She knew she should take her hand away, but she didn't.

"To tell you the truth, I'm not so sure anymore. Our relationship developed so quickly. Maybe too quickly. We seem to have drifted apart since I left the beach."

"But she's here now."

This time Colleen did take her hand away. "She only came when she heard about my case. Seems she knew the dead woman in college. It's strange. Gillian knew Candy Emerson and now I find out she knew Sheila Cunningham too. She was romantically involved with both."

"An odd coincidence, but you're not thinking she's somehow involved?"

"No, but it makes me uncomfortable."

"Have you talked to her about it?"

Colleen took a nervous sip of her espresso. "How did we get back on me? I want to know about you. What do you do for fun, besides protesting?"

"I don't have time for fun. But I make time when I have someone to share it with." The implication in her voice left no doubt about whom she was thinking.

Colleen stood. "I think I need to get going. I'll be right back." She headed for the ladies room.

* * * * *

Jenna watched the curvy redhead walk away from the table. Colleen's hair was like golden fire. Jenna had liked too the way the silk shirt made Colleen's ice-blue eyes more vivid. She had a nice body — shapely in all the right places. No social X-ray that one. Soft skin that made Jenna want to touch more than a hand. When Brian had asked her to dinner to meet Colleen, she'd almost decided not to go. It had been a long time since she'd felt any interest in one of the many women with whom her well-meaning friends set her up. By the evening's end, she'd known Colleen was different. Sensitive. Caring. Unpretentious. How lucky she was that Colleen's investigation had thrown them together again.

She called the waiter and paid the check, all the while hoping she hadn't scared Colleen. She wanted to get to know this woman, and not just as a business acquaintance. But just how much did Gillian figure in Colleen's life? She'd seemed very possessive Monday night at La Tomate, but from what Colleen said, Gillian spent most of her time at Rehoboth Beach. That was no way to keep a lady. Once Gillian returned to the beach, Jenna would have the advantage. And she intended to use it.

She smiled as Colleen returned. "It's too nice a night to go home right away. How about a walk?"

"I'd like that. Let's go to Lammas first. I want to buy the new issue of *Curve*."

It was a beautiful autumn night. A crisp chill in the air made everything seem clean and new. The hot hazy days of summer were nothing but a faded memory. This particular strip of 17th Street housed several gay businesses, and once they were outside,

Jenna took Colleen's hand, and was pleased when she didn't pull away. Lammas Women's Bookstore was just a couple of doors down from Trumpets. She reluctantly let go of Colleen's hand as they negotiated the narrow stairs up to the bookstore. She didn't recognize the woman behind the counter.

Jenna leaned against the wall, content to watch as Colleen perused the magazines. She liked the way Colleen's brow wrinkled when she concentrated, the lift of her mouth when she read something funny. Her profile was strong yet soft. The red-gold curls shimmered under the lights like a tropical sunset. Jenna could only imagine what it would be like to touch them, and she was determined to find out.

Colleen was different from Jenna's past lovers, who were usually fellow members of her various softball and volleyball teams. Sex with them had been more like participating in a wrestling match. Even in her last long-term relationship, making love was a contest to see who would come out on top. Jenna knew that making love with Colleen would be a new experience. The thought of it made her squirm in her tweed pants. It seemed to be getting awfully hot in the store.

"Colleen," Jenna called out, "are you about ready? It's kind of warm in here."

Colleen turned and smiled at her. It took her breath away. If she didn't know better, she'd think she was falling in love. Colleen paid for her purchases, also showing Jenna that she'd bought one of her recommended books. Outside, she took Colleen's hand once again.

They walked in silence for a while. Jenna didn't

want the evening to end. "Let's go for coffee," she said. "There's a great place up the street that a friend of mine owns, Jolt 'n' Bolt. They've got great desserts too."

"I don't really think I should. I've had a lovely evening, but I have to get home. I'm sure Gillian is wondering where I am."

The mention of Gillian brought Jenna back to reality. Colleen was involved with her; Jenna had no right to read more into their outing than a simple informational business dinner. She couldn't quite bring herself to let go of Colleen's hand, though, and felt her hold tighten.

"Yes, of course. I'll walk you home."

This time, Colleen did pull away. "I don't think that would be a good idea. I can catch a cab."

Jenna felt a disappointment so intense it was almost like a physical pain. What a fool she'd been. She resolved to resist her friends' future efforts to set her up with anyone. Or, at the very least, to find out if they were attached. What had Brian been thinking? He was Colleen's best friend. Surely he knew the situation with her and Gillian?

"I'll get one for you," Jenna said.

She hailed the next cab and saw Colleen safely inside. She insisted on paying. As the car pulled away, she had the feeling she'd never see Colleen again. Colleen turned and waved from the back seat. As the car disappeared around the corner, Jenna waved too and then called a cab of her own. Not willing to go home just yet, she directed the cabbie to drive to The Phase One. A little flirting and a couple of beers would lighten her mood, but she knew no woman there would compare to the Irish lass with red hair and blue eyes who had captured her heart.

Jenna looked kind of forlorn standing on the street corner all alone, and Colleen felt a pang of guilt. Guilt that she didn't want to leave Jenna and guilt that she did. How was it possible to have such strong feelings for two women at once?

Everything she'd been taught told her you loved one person and remained faithful. She hadn't done anything with Jenna except hold hands, but with the feelings in her heart she may as well have. Now she had to go home to Gillian and pretend nothing had happened. Well, nothing had, she told herself over and over again as the cab sped through the streets. Too quickly, her apartment building appeared before she knew it.

She sat in the back seat without moving. The driver finally turned to her. "You getting out, or what?"

She scrambled out without a word, wondering briefly if Jenna had remembered to tip the driver. Inside, she checked the mail, choosing to stand in the lobby and look through the envelopes and catalogs. Then she chatted a few moments with a neighbor on his way out.

Colleen realized she was delaying the inevitable. She took the stairs. By the time she got to her door, she was breathing heavily, whether from nerves or from being out of shape she didn't know. She heard movement inside the apartment as she turned her key in the lock. The door swung open.

"Where in the hell have you been?" Gillian demanded.

"Hi, Gillian." Normal-voiced, not shaky.

"I've been worried about you," Gillian said as she helped Colleen with her coat. "I know you were going back to the film studio and to see Roger. You didn't leave a message."

"I'm sorry." She kissed Gillian on the mouth. "I just haven't stopped all day."

Gillian returned her kiss. It sent the familiar current through Colleen's body. Gillian was holding her waist and pulling her closer. Their kiss deepened. Colleen thrust her fingers into Gillian's thick hair. She breathed in the scent of Gillian's cologne, felt the hard, muscled body mold into her own. Gillian clung to Colleen's waist, possessive and demanding. She roughly pulled the silk shirt from Colleen's pants and stopped their kiss only long enough to unbutton the shirt and unzip the pants. Her mouth possessed Colleen's again as she stripped Colleen naked and pushed her onto the couch.

Gillian was dressed only in a long, white T-shirt and white bikini underwear. It was her favorite lounging attire, and Colleen loved to see her in it. Now Colleen pulled the T-shirt off as they fell against the couch. She ran her hands over the sculpted body and cupped the full breasts. She moaned involuntarily as Gillian kissed her neck and bit her tenderly on the shoulder. Gillian's hands were all over her, her touch alternately soft and hard. Her whispered promises of what she was going to do sent shivers up Colleen's spine.

Later, as they lay tangled together, Gillian asked, "So, where were you all day?"

"Like I said, I had a lot to do. I interviewed the studio people again. They have a new actress who doesn't look old enough to be out of high school. I'm curious to find out just how old."

"And what will you do if you find out she's underage?"

"I don't know. I'm sure I could get advice from Jenna Bolden." She felt Gillian stiffen.

"You like her, don't you?"

"Well, yes. She's nice to be around. Why don't you like her?"

Gillian disentangled herself from Colleen's arms and sat up. She slipped her T-shirt back on. "It's not that I don't like her," she said, not looking at Colleen.

Colleen laughed and put her hand on Gillian's shoulder. "Don't tell me you're jealous? You don't have to worry about Jenna. I love you."

There. The words were out.

"I know you do," Gillian said as she leaned over and kissed Colleen's cheek. "And maybe I am a little jealous. She can see you anytime. I only get a weekend here and there."

Colleen noticed that Gillian did not say "I love you" back. "That's not my fault," she responded, a bit peeved. "I've asked you to come live with me."

"And I've asked you to come to the beach."

"It's not the same thing, and you know it. I have a job here. One that I like. You're the one with the money. You can live anywhere, with or without a job."

"Is that the real issue here? The money?"

Colleen pulled on her clothes. It was ludicrous to argue while naked, and she was annoyed that their love-making was spoiled. "You know that was never an issue with me. I don't think you're over Candy. You still love her, and I can't compete with a dead woman. And if someone else wants to pay attention to me while you keep me at arm's reach, I'll let her."

"Colleen, I didn't intend to fight with you. Of course I'm over Candy. And you're the one who helped me to do it." She reached for Colleen. "Come here, darling. We're so wonderful together. Let's not ruin it."

Reluctantly, Colleen let herself be drawn into Gillian's strong embrace. She had a hard time resisting Gillian's green eyes and engaging grin. If she was honest with herself, she'd admit that she was confused. She *did* have feelings for Jenna, but not the same as those for Gillian. If only Gillian were more committed, Colleen would gladly give her whole heart and soul. But despite what she might say, Colleen knew Gillian still held back. Those dark green eyes revealed a lot whenever Candy's name came up, and Colleen had seen the same look when she talked of Sheila Cunningham. Both women obviously had had a profound influence on Gillian's life, and Colleen could only hope that she might somehow banish the ghosts of Gillian's past.

"By the way," Gillian said, "I talked to Stephan tonight. He and Phillip are coming to D.C. for Halloween."

Colleen clapped her hands. "It'll be so good to see them. I'm surprised that Phillip is up to traveling."

"Ah, the wonders of modern medicine, and having a friend who can hire a limo."

"We'll let them have the bed. You and I can sleep on the floor with the cat."

"No need. I've booked them a room at the Ritz-Carlton."

Chapter Eleven

In the office Thursday morning, Colleen absently chewed on a pencil as she recalled her and Gillian's conversation from two nights before. She was trying to discern whether Gillian's money was indeed an issue with her. Her notes on the Cunningham case were spread across her desk. She had been trying to put them in order, but Gillian's talk of limos and booking expensive hotel rooms distracted her. Money had never been an issue for her before. Her parents lived a comfortable life and had provided well for all their children. Her brother was a successful civil engineer and her sister was a wife and mother married to a Navy pilot. Colleen made decent money at Sampson and Rhoades, with the potential to move up the corporate ladder. Was she actually jealous of Gillian's affluence?

"Problems with the case?" Lisa Anderson's voice startled her. Momentarily flustered, she dropped her pencil and made a semblance of trying to pull all the papers into a neat pile.

"No problems. Just thinking."

Lisa sat down and crossed her long legs. She wore a red linen suit with a cream silk blouse. The skirt was actually longer than usual. "Mr. Rhoades received a phone call from Roger Cunningham. Seems he's upset that one of our agents has been harassing him."

Colleen felt a hot flash of annoyance. "That's not true. I merely questioned him about his relationship with his daughter. I think I was out to see him twice."

Lisa waved her hand in dismissal. "Don't worry about it. I took care of it with Mr. Rhoades. He's easily influenced at times when big money is involved, and I guess Cunningham has lots of it?"

"That's putting it mildly. I looked him up in *Who's Who*. He made his money in foreign investments and smart stock market gambles. He was a millionaire by thirty." She paused. "Should I call him?"

"I took care of that too," Lisa said. "He was quite unpleasant on the phone. I'd like to give you to another assignment."

"You're taking me off the Starlight case?"

"No, but I thought you might be just about ready to wrap it up. Am I wrong?"

"Not really. I've found no evidence that Jackson Ramses or anyone else at the studio was responsible for Sheila's death. The police and autopsy reports certainly don't hint at any foul play."

"You don't seem satisfied."

"Maybe it's just that I have trouble believing someone of Sheila's means could have fallen so low. I mean, she had a rich father. Everything money could buy. How did she end up a washed-out porn actress on heroin?"

"It's not our job to try to explain or justify circumstances. We collect facts and determine whether someone is trying to cheat their insurance company. You're still new at this game. It takes time and experience to be able to distance yourself emotionally. Or maybe you feel a little let down after the excitement of the Emerson case?"

"Perhaps you're right. Give me a couple more days, and I'll have the final report on your desk. Can the new assignment wait until then?"

Lisa stood. "I'll E-mail you the particulars, but it can wait. Simple case. Man made his ferret his life insurance beneficiary. His relatives claim he was unduly influenced by the animal's vet, who happens to be the executor of the estate." She laughed.

Colleen laughed too and turned to her computer. She typed out her preliminary report. She listed the people she had spoken to and the information they'd given her, and summarized the police and autopsy reports. In her conclusion, she concurred with the police that there was no reason to suspect that Sheila

Cunningham had died of anything but an accidental overdose of a narcotic drug. Therefore, Franklin and Associates should pay Starlight Studios, Inc., the agreed-on sum.

As the report printed, Colleen leaned back in her chair. She was dissatisfied with the whole thing. It seemed too cut-and-dried. She hadn't uncovered anything to prove otherwise, yet she couldn't shake the feeling that she was missing something. She sensed that Bob Jones held the key, but she didn't know how to find him. She'd spent part of yesterday trying to track him down. The address and phone number Jackson Ramses had provided were useless. A search using Internet resources hadn't turned up anything either, nor had a call to his union.

The shrill ring of the phone startled her. "Fitzgerald here."

Silence.

"Is anyone there?"

"Hello?" The voice was soft, hesitant. Like a child's.

"This is Colleen Fitzgerald."

More silence.

"I'm going to hang up. Who is this?"

"My name is Angela."

Colleen had to strain to hear the voice. "How can I help you?"

"I need to talk to you. Can we meet?"

"What's this about?"

"Not on the phone. Meet me at Starbucks in an hour."

"Wait a minute. Which Starbucks? Who are you?"

Nothing but the dial tone. Colleen hung up slowly. Given the number of Starbucks cafés in the city, she had no idea which one the caller wanted her to go to. The one at DuPont Circle was Colleen's usual choice, but there was also one just three blocks away from her office. The fact that the caller picked Starbucks made Colleen inclined to believe she knew Colleen's habits, which would make the DuPont café the logical choice. It also seemed logical the caller wanted to talk about the Sheila Cunningham case because it was the only one she was working on. She'd bet a day's salary the caller was the new actress on *Bad Moon Rising*. The childlike voice certainly supported that conclusion.

Colleen pulled her report from the printer and glanced through it. If the caller did have new information, this report was not yet finished. She crumpled it up and threw it in the trash.

She pulled on her coat and headed out into the clear October day. There was a pronounced chill in the air. Dead leaves crackled under her feet. Chrysanthemums lent a splash of fading color here and there. The air smelled fresh and clean. She wished she'd remembered to wear her gloves. Tempted to walk, she motioned for a cab and hoped she'd picked the right Starbucks.

In mid-morning, the popular café was not too crowded. Colleen picked a stool and table near the window for the dual purpose of people-watching and identifying her visitor, whoever that might be. She ordered her usual and settled down to wait. Because she wasn't sure this particular Starbucks was the right one, she decided she'd wait no longer than an hour. Half an hour later, Colleen was wondering if she shouldn't leave when a familiar-looking blonde approached the entrance. She appeared nervous, and it took Colleen a few minutes to realize that she was indeed the young Starlight actress. Afraid the girl might change her mind, Colleen bolted from her stool and met her at the door.

"Hello. I'm Colleen. Are you coming to meet me?" The girl looked frightened and ready to run. Colleen took her arm gently and led her inside.

"Can I get you something to drink? A hot chocolate, maybe?"

Though still visibly tense, the girl smiled and shrugged off her jean jacket. "Thanks, but I prefer coffee. A mocha latte would be nice."

Colleen was hesitant to leave her alone, afraid she might still leave. "You won't go anywhere, will you?"

"No, I promise."

Colleen went to order two lattes, keeping an eye on the girl the whole time. Seeing as how the girl was so skinny, she also bought two chocolate croissants. She put everything down and pushed one latte and both pastries across the table.

"You called me?" Colleen asked.

"Yes."

"I wasn't sure this was the right Starbucks. How did you pick this one?"

The girl took a bite of a croissant. "Bob Jones told me."

"Bob Jones? You're in touch with him? I've been trying to track him down for days."

"He's hiding out in some motel. He left the company because he says someone tried to kill him. He wants to find out who."

Colleen was speechless. This was news to her. She wondered why he hadn't contacted her. She watched the girl, who ate as if she hadn't had a bite in days. She was pathetically thin, but the bloom of youth still sparkled in her blue eyes and blushed her cheeks. Her blonde hair was thick and wavy and appeared natural. Her lips were full and rosy. Her collarbones protruded through the thin pink T-shirt adorned with Disney's Cinderella. Her breasts were neither too large nor too small. At this moment, she certainly didn't look like a porn actress, yet Colleen could only assume that was what she was. After all, she had seen her at the studio, and Jackson Ramses had talked about a replacement for Amber Rose.

"You're Angela."

The girl licked her fingers and took a deep gulp of her latte. "That was so delicious. Thank you. Yes, I'm Angela White. I even get to keep that as my stage name."

"How old are you, Angela?"

The girl was immediately wary. "Old enough."

Colleen reached over and took her hand. Angela tried to pull away, but Colleen held fast. "I'm not the enemy. You called me, remember? Tell me the truth, how did you wind up on the set of this video?"

Angela suddenly appeared on the verge of tears. "I met Mr. Ramses at a McDonald's soon after I got here. He said he'd take care of me, that he'd teach me all about the movie business. He was so sweet to me, and so good-looking. At first he just wanted me to be a stand-in for poor Amber, but then he planned to replace her with me."

"You don't have to stay with him, you know. I can help. This is no life for a young girl like you. You're not nineteen, are you?"

Angela hesitated. Colleen could see indecision play across her face. Then she took a deep breath. "No, I'm sixteen. Back home, all the kids got fake I.D."

"And where is home?"

"Hopewell, Virginia. It's near Richmond. I ran away 'cause I couldn't take it anymore. My father left and my mother took up with some creep. He kept looking at me in a way that made my skin crawl. I was afraid of him."

Feeling a surge of anger, Colleen replied, "Don't you realize this life is just as bad, if not worse? You know what happened to Amber Rose."

This time Angela managed to pull her hand away. Her mouth tightened into a thin line. "I don't need you preaching at me. Bob said you would help me."

"I'm sorry. You're right. What do you want me to do?"

"I don't want to be in this movie, but I signed a contract. Jackson says if I don't do it, I owe him money, and I don't have a dime."

"That's B.S. He can find someone else."

"He says he can't, not someone like me. I'm still a virgin." This time the tears fell. "He says people love movies where a girl gets laid for the first time. He wants me to do it with Chris, but he's scary and so big."

Colleen felt a rage well up in her unlike any other. In that instant, all she wanted to do was to kill Jackson Ramses. She felt the tears in her own eyes and angrily rubbed them away. She determined she would never let this girl near him again.

"You are *not* going back to the studio. Don't worry about Jackson Ramses. I'll take care of him. Let's go."

Still crying, Angela held Colleen's hand as they left the café. Colleen hailed a cab and had the driver take them to her apartment. Gillian was home, seated at Colleen's little breakfast table and working on the computer. She looked up in apparent surprise as they walked through the door.

"Gillian, I'm so glad you're home. This is Angela White, and she'll be staying with us for a while."

When Gillian heard the key in the lock, she was surprised. Colleen rarely came home in the middle of the day. And when Colleen came through the door with a blonde woman in tow, Gillian felt herself stiffen with shock.

For a moment, it was as if Sheila had come back to life. A young, beautiful Sheila. She stood behind Colleen, big blue eyes bright with tears. The blonde hair tumbled in disarray around her face, resting on shoulders that were much too thin. Gillian felt as if she'd stepped back in time. She saw Sheila once again at the playground, needing her help.

She abandoned the computer. She'd been trying to write an article on the new professional women's basketball leagues, but couldn't seem to concentrate. She could only think of Sheila and how their lives had diverged so greatly. She had wondered too about her feelings for Colleen. That she had them and they were strong was not in question, but was it love? Just why was she so reluctant to make a commitment, to move from Rehoboth to the city? And how much were her feelings for Candy Emerson still influencing her life?

It was true that Colleen had come into her life suddenly and that her feelings had grown quickly.

Gillian surprised herself too by liking Colleen's body so much. As a fitness fanatic, Gillian usually had nothing but disdain for those who didn't take care of themselves in the same way. Yes, it was true that Colleen had tried the aerobics route, but Gillian could tell she'd given that up. Still, she liked the soft body with the curves in all the right places. It was so different from Candy's rock-hard bodybuilder's physique. Making love with Colleen seemed perfect. She was responsive and loving.

She hadn't really come to any conclusions, except that maybe she should stop processing so much and just let her relationship with Colleen progress on its own. One thing she did know — she couldn't take things for granted. Jenna Bolden seemed to have made quite an impression on Colleen. If Gillian wasn't careful, Colleen might switch her affections, and Gillian was determined not to let that happen.

"Angela . . . Hello . . . Are you a relative of Colleen's?" Gillian heard her own voice trembling.

"Why don't you go take a nice hot shower," Colleen said as she pushed Angela toward the bathroom. She stopped and pulled a sweater and a pair of jeans from her dresser. "Here are some clean clothes too."

When the girl disappeared into the bathroom, Colleen said, "This must be quite a shock to you."

"What do you mean?"

"C'mon, Gillian. I see the resemblance to Sheila. She's supposed to be Sheila's replacement on the video, but she's underage and I can't let her go back there."

Gillian laughed nervously. "Did you rescue her on your white steed?"

122

"She called me. You remember the production assistant I told you about? Bob Jones? Seems he's hiding out in a motel somewhere 'cause someone tried to kill him. Or so he claims. Well, he gave Angela my number and she met me at the Starbucks on DuPont. That's where I'd met him too."

"What are you going to do with her?"

"That despicable man, Jackson Ramses, picked her up at a fast food place. Told her he'd make her a star. Little did she know just what kind of star."

"Well, you read about that sort of thing happening all the time — guys on the lookout for runaways to recruit them into lives as prostitutes." She lowered her voice as the water in the shower shut off. "Do you think she's on drugs?"

"I didn't see any signs of it. She only arrived here about three weeks ago. How convenient for Starlight. They lose their big star and have a young novice waiting in the wings to take over. It certainly gives them at least one motive to get rid of Sheila."

Angela came out of the bathroom just then. Dressed in Colleen's too-big clothes, she looked vulnerable and young. She toweled her hair vigorously. "It feels so good to be clean."

"Angela," Colleen said, "I've got to get back to the office. Gillian will take care of you."

Gillian looked at Colleen. She didn't want to sit around and babysit all day. If Colleen knew Gillian was not happy, she gave no sign of it. Instead, she motioned Gillian to the tiny kitchen.

"I need to make some calls, and I can't do it here." She kissed Gillian lightly on the cheek. "I tell you what. I'll call Jenna first. I'm sure she knows someone who can take Angela off our hands. You wouldn't want her returning to Jackson Ramses, would you?"

"Of course not."

"See what you can find out." She kissed Gillian again, this time on the lips, teasing with her tongue. Gillian grabbed her arms, feeling the urge to put Colleen on the tiny table and have her right then and there. Colleen pushed her away, laughing. "Not now, sweetie. I'll be home as soon as possible."

In the living room, Angela sat on the sofa petting Smokey. He curled contentedly in her lap, his purrs loud.

"You'll never get rid of him," Colleen said to Angela. "I'll be back soon."

When Colleen left, Gillian felt trapped, but it wasn't as if she'd been planning to go somewhere. The magazine article she'd been writing was due in two weeks. She paced the room, glancing at Angela on the couch, still unnerved by her looks. Her imagination began running wild, thinking this girl could be Sheila's long-lost child. But that was impossible. It would mean Sheila had been fourteen when she was pregnant, and Gillian knew that certainly wasn't true. And besides, Colleen had told her that Sheila'd had a boy.

"It's awfully nice of you to let me stay here."

Gillian stopped pacing and sat on an easy chair that faced the couch. "Is that whole story you told Colleen true?"

"Yes. Why would you think I'd lie?"

"Oh, I don't know. A play on someone's sympathies? Looking for a free place to stay? Maybe you're a little spy."

Angela didn't seem upset by Gillian's insinuations, but kept stroking the cat. The motion was almost hypnotic. "I only called Colleen because Bob told me she would help me. I didn't want to be in that movie. Jackson took me in. Promised he'd make me a star. I didn't know what kind of movies he was talking about. Honest."

Gillian didn't believe for a minute that Angela was as naive as she seemed, but she decided not to confront her. "Were you there when Sheila died?"

"Sheila? Was that Amber's real name? Nice. I wasn't on the set that day. Well, I'd been there earlier, but that crazy guy was there and he frightened me. They laugh and call him Ravin' Randy. He kept telling us we were going to rot in hell."

"When you found out what Jackson did for a living, why'd you stay?"

"Where was I supposed to go?" It was practically a wail. Smokey jumped off her lap in panic. The girl started crying. "I didn't know anyone in the city, and I'd run out of money."

Tears always made Gillian nervous. "I'm sorry. I can't imagine what it must have been like. Tell me what you know about Sheila's death."

Her eyes still shining with tears, Angela took a deep breath and hiccuped. Even with a red nose and red-rimmed eyes, she was still pretty. She sniffed a couple of times. Gillian handed her a tissue. She took another breath.

"Like I said, I'd left the set. Jackson had a cab take me to the motel where we were staying. Things weren't going well that day. Jackson was yelling at

Amber a lot, telling her he was replacing her with me. Hobie had been by earlier. He was her dealer. I think she'd had a fight with him too."

"Wait a minute. You mean to tell me this guy blatantly comes on the set and sells drugs? To the others too?"

"To some. It makes them relax. The drugs, I mean. I tried pot once with Jackson, but I didn't like it. My mama didn't raise me to be that way. She said drugs were evil."

"But you ran away from home and hung out with pornographers. How do you think your mother would feel about that?" Gillian's voice was harsh.

Angela turned away and buried her face in a pillow. "I don't want to talk anymore," came her muffled reply.

"Fine. I have work to do."

Gillian left the girl crying into the pillow and returned to her computer. The words of her article swam together. She couldn't concentrate, and didn't like the anger she was feeling or the idea that Angela was to blame for her situation. It connected her to Sheila, to the choices Sheila had made. Gillian resented her college sweetheart. Resented her for all the unresolved feelings, for the helplessness Gillian had felt when Sheila disappeared. Gillian didn't like feeling out of control. And right now, that was exactly how she felt.

Colleen didn't feel comfortable leaving Angela and Gillian alone — there seemed to be a strange tension in the air. But she couldn't make the phone calls she needed to make with Angela listening. Colleen could only hope everything would be okay.

Her first call was to Jenna Bolden. As Colleen knew she would be, Jenna was horrified to find out that Angela was underage. She did indeed know someone who could take the girl in. Jenna didn't want to contact Social Services where she knew Angela would become just another statistic and probably end up on the street again. If she or someone in her group couldn't reunite Angela with her family, they would take care of her. In response to Colleen's question of filing charges against Starlight, Jenna told her that if Angela did have fake I.D., Jackson Ramses had not knowingly broken the law. Federal regulations require adult film producers to obtain two forms of picture I.D. from each actor, photocopies of which are signed and placed with the contract.

Colleen then called several motels in the Southeast D.C. area to see if any of them had a Bob Jones registered. She was not surprised to find out they did not. He was either using an assumed name or staying in one of the other hundreds of motels in D.C. or its suburbs. A quick check with the police department verified that he had not filed any kind of complaint about a threat on his life. Tempted to go to the studio and confront Jackson Ramses, Colleen knew it would be foolish and she'd likely wind up in trouble herself.

She headed to Lisa Anderson's office. Colleen just might not be able to take the ferret case after all. Lisa was on the phone, a wedding catalog spread out on the desk. She did not sound happy, and slammed the phone down as Colleen hovered in the doorway. Lisa motioned her inside.

"I can't believe this. My wedding is a scant two weeks away and the stupid bridal shop has lost my veil. They can't get another one in time. How long does it take to put together some lace and tulle, for Christ's sake?"

Colleen didn't think it appropriate for Lisa to be doing wedding planning on company time, but it was not her place to say anything. She could only nod in sympathy.

"Sorry if I came at a bad time. I've had a development in the Cunningham case I thought you should know about. I have at my apartment a girl — sixteen, to be exact — who was to be Amber Rose's substitute on the video. It's possible the producer killed Sheila so he could use this girl instead."

"You've got to be kidding?" The incredulous look on Lisa's face was almost comical.

"I need a little more time to close the case."

"You know, it's not your job to solve murders. I think you should take this information to the police and let them do their job. As long as there are any suspicions, Franklin doesn't have to pay a dime."

"I guess you're right. I just feel personally involved."

"That is something you'll have to change. You can't get personal." She must have seen something in Colleen's face. "Okay, I'll give you one more week. Send me a preliminary today, but I expect your final report on my desk next Thursday afternoon."

Lisa picked up the phone. Their meeting was over. Colleen returned to her office and modified her earlier preliminary report, which she then E-mailed to Lisa. She didn't want to call the police just yet. She had just five more days to crack this case, not counting the weekend. It was time to talk to Rick Ewing again, and even Randy Wilson.

Chapter Twelve

Colleen called Jenna at work. She wanted to go to the studio again, but she wanted someone with her. Besides, Jenna would have the clout of the law behind her. They agreed to meet at the warehouse.

It was pretty quiet when Colleen arrived by cab. The yellow police tape was finally gone from Sheila's trailer, but the memorial of flowers remained. Someone had removed them from the steps, and they lay in a wilted heap on the asphalt. Colleen tentatively tried the door to the trailer and was surprised to find it open. She entered cautiously.

The stench made her gag. Cigarettes, vomit, cheap cologne, urine, alcohol, and who knew what else all combined to make a potent elixir of misery, hopelessness, and death. Just ahead of her, the faded chalk outline of a body showed where Amber Rose had ended her life. Fingerprint powder covered a nearby table and the boom box that sat on top. Curious, she pushed the play button, and Melissa Etheridge's throaty voice filled the silence.

Dust covered every surface, which explained why more fingerprint powder wasn't in evidence. She would have sworn no one had cleaned the place in years. The threadbare carpet throughout was ominously stained. Dirty dishes in the tiny kitchen grew science experiments any aspiring biologist would be proud to own. Someone had left the refrigerator door slightly open, and all inside had rotted too.

The bedroom and bathroom were only slightly less filthy, but looked as if someone had been searching for something. Clothes were strewn about, and jars on the dresser were left open. The sheets were off the bed, and even the mattress was moved. Was this the work of the police or someone else?

In the bedside table, Colleen found a few personal items. She smiled when she read the title of a popular lesbian romance novel. There were a couple of cheap rings, a gold chain with a crucifix, and a small photo album.

Colleen turned the plastic pages slowly. She saw a small, laughing girl holding an Easter basket and dressed in a frilly dress similar to the Easter outfits Colleen's mom used to sew for her. As the album progressed, the girl grew up. In one photo, Colleen recognized Roger Cunningham with Sheila. She assumed the other woman in the photo was Sheila's mother. They looked very much alike.

Then suddenly, Gillian looked out at her, dressed in what appeared to be a track outfit. The hair was a little longer, but Colleen would recognize that face and engaging grin anywhere. The next photo showed Gillian with Sheila. Their arms were around each other and they looked as if they had just kissed. An eerie feeling came over Colleen, and she could feel the hairs on her neck prickle. There were no more photos of Gillian, just a couple more of Sheila with different people. The last one was of an infant wrapped in a blue blanket. So, Sheila's baby *had* been a boy. Colleen took the photo out and looked at the back. Written in fading black ink were a date and height and weight, but no name. Colleen put the photo back and slipped the album into her purse.

Back in the living room, Colleen realized she'd found no evidence of drugs, but she was sure the police would have taken that. She looked around once more, wondering if Starlight Studios ever intended to clean it up. The trailer and all it stood for was the sad final chapter to Sheila's tragic life story.

She left the trailer and was happy to see that Jenna had arrived. So had Randy Wilson. As she approached, Colleen could tell he'd once been attractive. They liked them that way in Hollywood, even the Hollywood on the other side of the tracks. After seeing Randy the first time, she'd stopped by the Pleasure Palace and found copies of some of his videos, both gay and straight. The photos on the video boxes boasted a bodybuilder's physique and the inevitable blonde hair and blue eyes. He'd smiled out at her from the box with an irresistible and mischievous grin.

The Randy Wilson before her now was thinner; his clothes hung shapelessly. The blonde hair was lank and greasy. The disease had taken its toll, but he seemed energetic. He and Jenna were involved in a heated discussion.

"I have every right to be here," he was saying, "especially now since Amber's death. Don't you see, everything I've been saying is true." He pointed to his Bible. " 'For all the nations have drunk the wine of the wrath of her fornication. The kings of the earth have committed fornication with her, and the merchants of the earth have become rich through the abundance of her luxury.' "

"We both want the same thing, to put an end to this. But your way is too antagonistic. Telling these people they're going to hell doesn't accomplish anything."

"Hello you two," Colleen said.

Randy gave her a scowl. Jenna came over and gave her a kiss on the cheek. "Where have you been?"

"In the trailer. I wanted to look around." She turned to Randy and held out her hand. "I'm Colleen Fitzgerald. We haven't meet, but I know you're Randy Wilson."

He refused to shake her hand. "What do you want?"

"Just to talk a bit. I understand you used to be an actor?"

"That was before I found the light, but God still punishes me." His voice was bitter. "I have the scourge that is AIDS. 'Vengeance is mine: I will repay, sayeth the Lord.' "

"I'm sorry to hear that. Do you blame Starlight?"

"I can only blame myself, but they — and others like them — are the insidious worm that invades our spiritual psyche. They must all repent and give up their evil ways. 'For the wages of sin is death, but the gift of God is eternal life in Christ Jesus our Lord.' "

Colleen looked at Jenna and then back at Randy. "Did you kill Amber?"

He surprised her by laughing. It shook his thin body and brought an animated sparkle to his pale blue eyes. "I did not kill her, but neither did she kill herself. It was all of them. Hobie. Jackson. Chris."

Colleen didn't think the parking lot beside a warehouse was the best place to conduct business, but she didn't want to interrupt when Randy seemed willing to talk.

"Are you talking about a conspiracy?" She was beginning to feel a little like Fox Mulder.

He stopped laughing and glared at her. "Do you think I'm an idiot? I'm talking figuratively. They all brought her down. She's better off dead. And now that evil man has a new innocent to corrupt, but I can save her. I *will* save her!"

"If you're talking about Angela White," Jenna cut in, "she's safe. She won't be back on the set."

"Randy," Colleen said, "you hang around here a lot. You must know everyone. Did you ever see this man?" She took the album from her purse and opened it to Roger's photo.

He squinted at the picture. "Seems familiar. Is that Amber with him? Who is it?"

"Her father." She put the album away. "You think you know him?"

"I didn't say that. Seems familiar, that's all." He laughed again. "Maybe he was one of my co-stars."

Colleen handed him her card, as did Jenna. "If you think of anything that might be useful, please call one of us. I'm going to talk to Jackson Ramses. Are you coming, Jenna?"

"You tell that scum there's a spot in hell waitin' for him. And I'll be right behind to push him in," Randy called as Colleen and Jenna walked to the warehouse entrance. " 'The Lord is known by the judgment He executes; the wicked shall be turned in to hell.' "

"You think there's any chance at all he was involved in Sheila's death?" Colleen asked as they entered the dark building. She was surprised to find it open.

"My instincts say no. He's just a bitter, sick man. As an activist in the last couple of years, I have met both men and women who tell stories about pornography and the devastating impact it has had on their lives. I've seen it with my law practice too."

"Just how binding is that contract Angela signed?"

"If she's a minor, nothing she signed is legally binding without a parent or guardian's signature too."

Colleen took a deep breath as she pushed open the door to the studio. It was quiet and empty. She could see the set and cameras, but no one occupied them.

"They must have wrapped," Jenna said.

"Finished the video? How could they, without Angela?"

Jenna approached the king-size bed and briefly picked up a corner of the red sheet. Her nose wrinkled with distaste. "I suppose it's possible that Ramses gave them the day off. I'm surprised the door would be unlocked. This is expensive camera equipment."

"As a matter of fact, I did shut down for the day." Colleen and Jenna both started at the sound of Ramses' voice. He'd come from the office. "Now, why are you here?"

Jenna put on her most authoritative, legal voice. And Colleen had to admit, she did look imposing in her sharply cut burgundy suit and no-nonsense white blouse. "We're here about Angela White. You are in serious legal trouble, Mr. Jackson."

He gazed at them calmly. "I don't know who you're talking about."

"Oh, come on, Jackson," Colleen said. "I saw her here the other day. Remember? I threatened to find out how old she really was unless you let me talk to your crew."

"What about her?"

"She's underage and you were going to put her in a sex video," Jenna said evenly.

"I have documented proof that all my employees are eighteen or older. I'd be happy to show you my files." He waved in the direction of his office.

"You are some piece of work." Jenna didn't bother to hide her contempt.

"Look," he replied, "this is a business like any other. I produce a product that is in demand. If consenting adults choose to purchase that product for whatever reason, well . . ."

"Are you married, Mr. Ramses?" Colleen asked.

"No. Why?"

"I just wondered how you'd feel if you found out your sixteen-year-old daughter was in porn films."

He rolled his eyes in exasperation. "I've told you everything I know. There's nothing left to tell. Amber was an addict. She got some pure stuff, and it killed her. End of story."

Colleen said, "I think you got rid of Sheila so you could replace her with Angela. Or maybe with all the production cost overruns you needed the cash. All I need is suspicion of wrongdoing to hold up that insurance money, and you'll be tied up in legal proceedings for so long you'll never make another video."

"I'm going to tell you one more time. I did not kill Amber, nor did anyone else on my crew. This is a business. If I want an actress off of a video, I fire her, I don't kill her. Talk to her damn supplier. Ask him where he got the stuff."

"Tell me where to find him."

Jackson laughed, a harsh bitter sound. "You're not going to his neighborhood, lady. They'll chew you up and spit you out. Hang around here a day or two. He always comes crawling out from under his rock sooner or later. You've got Angela now. Leave me alone."

He turned to walk away. Colleen wanted to slap his handsome face. She came closer to feeling hatred than she ever had before, even though it was not something she'd been taught at home, either from her parents or the church.

Jenna must have seen something in her face

because she came and put her arms around her. Colleen liked the feeling. "He's not worth it. Let me take you home. You said you left Angela with Gillian? I'm sure she's tired of babysitting by now."

They walked out of the warehouse. It was already getting dark. Colleen wondered where the day had gone. She loved the autumn, but sometimes it depressed her too because the days grew short. Halloween would see the end of daylight saving time and the start of the long winter, even though winter didn't officially begin until December. The parking lot was empty but for a metallic silver Lexus.

Jenna took Colleen's arm. "I have my car. I'll drive you to your apartment."

Jenna drove expertly and quickly through the streets, despite the rush-hour traffic. She could not find parking near Colleen's apartment building so they had to walk several blocks. The whole time, they kept their silence. Colleen didn't know what Jenna was thinking, but her own thoughts were a swirl of confusion.

After her discussion with Angela, Gillian sat at her laptop and stared at the screen. She'd lost her whole train of thought. She couldn't even remember the names of the women's basketball teams she was supposed to be writing about. She glanced over at the couch. The girl lay slouched in one corner, her eyes closed. She looked even younger and more vulnerable than she had before. The cat had returned and lay curled in her lap. Gillian decided she'd been a bit harsh with her. She closed her file and shut down the computer.

"Sleeping?" Gillian asked as she approached the couch.

Angela stirred and opened her eyes. They were still red from crying. "Not really. Just thinking."

Gillian sat next to her. "I'm sorry for being so rude before. I know you're looking for help, not lectures."

"I guess I deserve it. My mother and I had a silly fight and I ran away to teach her a lesson. I'm the one who got the lesson."

"Does she know you're okay?"

Angela started crying again. "Jackson wouldn't let me call."

Gillian wished Colleen was there. She didn't want to just let Angela use the phone. What if her disappearance was registered with the Center for Missing and Exploited Children? They could trace the call, send the police to the apartment, and then they'd all be in trouble. Angela continued to cry quietly. Gillian pulled her close and put her arms around her. Angela was so thin, mere bones. Gillian stroked the beautiful blonde hair that was so much like Sheila's. It smelled like Colleen's, but evoked memories of another blonde. Memories of a laughing young woman who introduced Gillian to the wonders of real lesbian love. Gillian tightened her hold on Angela.

Angela had stopped crying. She snuggled into Gillian's arms, sniffling occasionally. Gillian made a decision.

"I think you should call your mom."

Angela sat up and pushed away from Gillian, her blue eyes wide with dismay. "I can't do that. She'd kill me."

"You know that's not true. She's probably sick with worry." Gillian held the phone out to her, but she didn't move. "You don't have to tell her where you are. Just that you're safe."

"What if Jackson finds me?"

"He won't. A good friend of Colleen's is going to help you. She's a lawyer, and she'll take care of Jackson Ramses. Now, come on, dry your eyes and get on the phone."

Angela smiled then, and to Gillian it was the most beautiful sight in the world. She pulled the phone close and dialed. Gillian went to the kitchen to give her some privacy.

About ten minutes later, Angela joined her in the kitchen. Her eyes were sparkling, and this time not from tears. "Thanks so much, Gillian. She was so happy. All she wants is for me to come home. She even dumped that creepy boyfriend."

"I can make the arrangements, if you'd like, and you won't have to take the bus this time. Now, where is home?"

"Hopewell, Virginia."

"If you'd prefer, I can fly your mother here. Well, let's wait to see what Jenna has to say."

Gillian decided to take Angela shopping. She surprised herself by enjoying the activity. Gillian usually hated shopping, but had to admit it was fun to watch Angela pick out clothes and then ask Gillian's opinion. They returned home with numerous shopping bags and Gillian's credit card having seen more activity in a few hours than it had in weeks.

When they returned to the apartment, Gillian sat down once again at the computer. She didn't work on her basketball article, but drafted one about Sheila and the life she had fallen into. She knew she'd have to do a lot more research, but she would write an article to educate girls like Angela. For the first time in a long while, Gillian felt excited about her work.

When the key finally turned in the lock, Gillian had learned quite a lot from surfing the Internet. She'd decided to write a series of articles, starting with the one of Sheila's life story. She shut everything down and went to the door. Angela sat on the couch, playing with Smokey and channel surfing. She'd changed into one of her new outfits.

Colleen came through the door, followed by Jenna. She looked tired.

Chapter Thirteen

Colleen *was* tired. She only wanted to take a long, hot shower and then nestle into soft blankets and Gillian's arms while she watched TV and ate Jiffy Pop. Instead, she had a teenager to contend with, one who she hoped would leave with Jenna. She felt a twinge of guilt at her thoughts.

She pushed open the door and was greeted by a beaming Gillian. Their kiss was long and deep. She didn't care that Jenna and Angela stood watching. She only cared that she was held tight within Gillian's strong arms. Her hands followed the muscular lines of Gillian's back, then reached down to caress her firm ass. She felt her heart beat faster and her breath quicken.

Laughing, Gillian finally pushed her gently away. "I'm so glad you've missed me," she whispered in Colleen's ear.

Colleen turned to Angela. Surprised to see her dressed in new clothes, she raised her eyebrows in question.

"I took Angela shopping," Gillian said. "It was too nice a day to stay cooped up here."

Jenna introduced herself to Angela and held out her hand. "I'm going to be helping you."

"Gillian's been telling me about you. I appreciate all of you taking me in like this. I feel really foolish about having run away." She smiled and took a deep breath. "I've already talked to my mom, and she wants me to come home. She's not with that guy anymore."

"Why, that's marvelous," Colleen said.

Angela came to Gillian and smiled up at her. "Gillian said she'd pay for me to go home or my mom to come here." Angela's face had that adoring look that could only mean she'd developed quite a crush on Gillian.

Colleen felt a quick bite of jealousy and quickly repressed it. The girl was all of sixteen, for crying out loud. If Gillian knew of Angela's feelings, she gave no sign. Jenna, however, was smiling with amusement.

"I think it would be better if your mother came here," Jenna said. "In the meantime, I'm taking you to a safe house. You want to pack up your new things?"

"Do I have to leave?" Angela's voice was almost a whine.

"I really don't have room here," Colleen said firmly. "Now, go on, pack your stuff."

Angela and Jenna left loaded down with shopping bags. Finally, Colleen and Gillian were alone. Colleen put her arms around Gillian and pulled her head down for another kiss. She really did love this woman, and she decided she'd take her any way she could get her. If that meant living in separate locales, then so be it. Seeing Gillian once or twice a month was better than not seeing her at all. She stepped back and looked into Gillian's deep green eyes. A rush of memories spilled through her — that first glimpse at Bodies By the Beach, the enticing look at Square One, their first moonlit walk along the beach that had led to a night of ecstasy.

"I've really missed you," Colleen said.

Gillian held her gently. "I know you want me to move to the city . . ."

Colleen held her fingers to Gillian's lips. "I don't want to pressure you in any way. Let's not talk serious now. I just want to make love with you."

Gillian smiled that rakish grin Colleen loved so much. Her grip on Colleen tightened. "Now, that's the kind of talk I like to hear." Her kiss took Colleen's breath away.

Later, in the darkness, Colleen and Gillian lay tangled together. Colleen's small night-light cast a faint bluish glimmer against one wall. For once, the apartment was quiet — no clomping footsteps from the upstairs neighbors, no screaming kids from the apartment next door, no grocery carts rattling in the outside hallway. If Colleen didn't know better, she'd think it was past midnight, but she knew it must only be around eight. Her whole body felt good. Gillian knew exactly how to make her quiver with pleasure. She stretched and kissed Gillian's damp neck.

"You want more?" Gillian murmured as she brushed her hand across Colleen's belly and down between her legs once again.

Laughing, Colleen pushed her hand gently away. "Actually, I am famished. You must be too."

"Only for you, my dear. Only for you."

"I love you so much."

"I'll take you to dinner," Gillian said as she sat up and pulled on a T-shirt. "Shower first?"

Colleen felt a deep pang of disappointment. Why did Gillian always change the subject when love entered the conversation? Weren't at least some of the feelings mutual? Gillian couldn't make love to her the way she did if she only had casual feelings. Or could she?

"You go first," Colleen said, hoping her voice didn't betray her disappointment. Now was not the time to talk about it. She didn't want to ruin their lovemaking, but couldn't admit that for her it was already tainted.

They ended up at Food for Thought. Since the restaurant had recently introduced a second menu for nonvegetarians, Colleen felt more comfortable bringing her carnivorous friends, and because it was Thursday night, the place wasn't too busy. They gave their orders to a purple-haired punkish waiter with multiple piercings and settled back to enjoy hot buttered cider. Gillian added rum to hers.

"Do you feel comfortable with Jenna having taken Angela?" Gillian asked.

"Of course. I don't have the room for an overnight guest that I'm not sleeping with. Jenna and her people will take good care of Angela. That was nice of you, by the way, to offer to pay her way home. And to buy all those clothes."

"I just want to do what I can. How's the case going? You about ready to wrap?"

"Angela puts a different spin on things. She was supposed to be Sheila's replacement. I think Jackson Ramses might have killed Sheila for the insurance money because he found Angela."

"C'mon, Colleen. That doesn't really make sense. And besides, he was in the warehouse when Sheila went to her trailer and overdosed."

"I'm not saying he injected her with the stuff himself. He could have substituted pure heroin for what she normally used. Or had someone else substitute it. Like this Hobie character."

"Have the police checked him out? The dealer? Surely they must have a rap sheet on him."

Colleen sighed. "You know, I haven't talked to them about him. Some kind of investigator I am, eh?"

Gillian smiled and placed her hand over Colleen's. "You've had a lot on your mind. And listen, I really don't think Jackson Ramses murdered Sheila just because he had some nubile young thing to take her place. It wouldn't make financial sense. Amber Rose was a hot commodity, if her video sales are any indication."

146

"How do you know about her video sales?"

"Just a little creative searching on the Web."

The waiter brought their food. Colleen took a bite, then said, "I don't think I'm going to find out what really happened. It's not such a cut-and-dried case like Candy's was. I guess what I'm afraid of most is that Sheila will just become another sad statistic in the drug war. I want someone to have killed her so she won't be blamed."

"Sheila was responsible for what happened to her. She was no naïve sixteen-year-old picked up at a bus station."

Colleen was surprised at the harsh tone. "Don't blame Sheila, Gillian. She's the victim here. Rejected by her father. Exploited by men like Jackson Ramses. Dying from drugs supplied by Hobie."

"Colleen, I think Jenna has influenced you too much. Sheila might not have had control over her father's rejection, but she certainly had choices about drugs and making sex movies like that. And before you give me that she-had-to-do-it-to-survive crap, let me remind you that she came from a wealthy family. She had a college education."

Colleen put her fork down. This was a Gillian she didn't know, and one that she didn't think she particularly liked. There was a real anger in her, and Colleen was determined to find out what the true problem was. "Gillian, you have no idea what her life was like after college. How many years had it been since you saw her? And what about the circumstances under which you saw her last? A badly beaten rape victim." Gillian refused to meet her eyes. "You're mad at her, aren't you? After all this time, you haven't forgiven her for rejecting you."

Gillian shoved her plate away, her lasagna barely touched. "You don't understand anything."

"You never resolved your feelings for Sheila. Is that why you won't get close to anyone? Why you won't let yourself love?"

Gillian rolled her eyes. "What? Are you my analyst now? You know nothing about me."

Colleen was angry too. "And that's exactly what our problem is. You keep me at arm's length. I know the superficial things. Your youthful rebellion. Your estrangement from your father. I now know of three women you've been involved with. You like the beach. You like fast cars. And you like seafood best."

"What do you want from me?"

"I want you to love me."

"I can't."

Colleen could swear she saw the hint of tears in Gillian's eyes. Her own tears threatened at Gillian's admission. "You can't? Or you won't?"

Gillian looked at Colleen then, her green eyes bright with unshed tears. Still always in control, Colleen thought. "You're partially right about Sheila. I did love her. When we broke up, we stayed friends, but it tore me apart to see her with other women. Oh, I certainly wasn't celibate." She laughed without humor. "But I never met anyone who mattered. Until Candy Emerson. She was the one who finally purged Sheila from my heart."

"So Candy's death was like losing Sheila all over again?"

Gillian gave a wry smile. "Maybe you *should* consider a career as a counselor." She took a sip of her cider. "The only thing that kept me going after Candy's death was meeting you. But I'm scared.

Scared of loving you like I loved them and then losing you."

Colleen took Gillian's hand. "The only way you'll lose me is if you keep pushing me away. I'm not trying to take Candy's place, or even Sheila's. Listen, maybe I've been pressuring you too much. Why don't we just enjoy our time together now?"

"I am, and I do. And I promise I'll make a decision soon about moving from Rehoboth." She sat in silence for a while, then said, "It's a nice night. How about a walk home?"

Colleen didn't really feel they'd resolved much, but she decided not to pursue it. At least, not at the moment. They paid the check and headed out the door and up Connecticut Avenue. The late-October chill was not unpleasant, especially when Gillian put her arm around her. They strolled along the avenue, occasionally stopping to look in a store window, then turned off Connecticut Avenue and walked up Colleen's street. She pointed out a carved pumpkin sitting on someone's porch, its toothy grin already lit with a candle. Someone was eager for Halloween.

"It's going to be great to see Phillip and Stephan again," Colleen said, thinking about them coming for Halloween. "I can't believe the progress Phillip has made on that protease cocktail in such a short time."

"Well, he's not out of the woods yet, but he certainly has a new chance. He's gained a few pounds and can almost walk without his cane."

"You know, you really don't have to pay for them to stay in a hotel. My place is small, but they're more than welcome."

Gillian took out her keys as they arrived at the apartment building. "You told Angela you didn't have room for her, remember? The guys will be more comfortable in the hotel, and it has a doctor on call." She held the door open for Colleen.

"Lisa has given me till next Thursday to wrap things up with the case. I still wish I could link Jackson Ramses to Sheila's death. I don't want him getting the money. Not terribly professional or objective, I know."

"Isn't it the studio that gets the money? Not Ramses himself?" Gillian asked as she followed Colleen into the elevator.

"But he's the producer. He's bankrolled the production, or at least gotten investors. He'd recoup his cost first."

"Honey, you have to get this man out of your mind."

Colleen knew Gillian would prefer to take the stairs, but six flights was hard for someone not in shape. She smiled apologetically as the elevator doors closed. Gillian immediately seized her, pushed her against the wall, and kissed her deeply. Colleen felt a thrill. It had always been a secret fantasy of hers to make love in an elevator, but that was the stuff for movies and novels. In less than two minutes, the doors opened to the sixth floor and Colleen broke away from Gillian, glancing guiltily into the hallway to be sure no one had seen them.

"A little paranoid, are we?" Gillian teased.

Colleen's mouth felt pleasantly bruised from Gillian's kiss, her body aroused. Heat rose in her face at Gillian's words. Her little homophobic gremlin was sitting on her shoulder again. She hated feeling like she had to hide. She got along with her neighbors and didn't want to do anything to change that. If she could be certain that other gay people lived in the building, she might not feel so alone, but that wasn't the situation, as far as she knew.

Smokey hurled himself at her legs and she automatically bent down to pet him. The light on her answering machine was blinking.

"Why don't you make us some decaf," Colleen said, "while I listen to my messages. It's probably Mom wanting me to housesit."

Gillian smiled wickedly. "That could be fun."

Colleen laughed. "Oh, no. You're not having me at my parents' house. I'd never be able to look them in the face again."

"Where's your sense of adventure?" Gillian asked from the tiny kitchen.

"Everywhere but Gaithersburg."

Colleen felt the doubt creep into her head. Internalized homophobia? It wasn't something she liked to admit to, but Gillian's teasing had inadvertently brought all that to the surface again. In February it would be a year since she'd moved to the city. She'd chosen the gay-friendly ambiance of the DuPont Circle area so she wouldn't feel paranoid about her sexuality, but the truth was that even there people were attacked in broad daylight for being gay. It was annoying and frustrating to have to play a role that wasn't truthful, but that's just the way it was. With a sigh, she pushed the button on her machine.

Beep. "Hi. It's Lisa. Listen, sorry to call you so late at home, but Mr. Ramses from Starlight called Mr. Rhoades and filed a formal complaint. Says you're harassing him. I explained what's going on, and Cranford is okay with it, but you've definitely got to

151

have this wrapped up soon. Try for Wednesday instead of Thursday."

Beep. "Hey, Colleen. It's Jenna. You're not gonna believe what happened. Bob Jones was found dead in his motel room. I heard it on the early news. Police don't think foul play is involved. Something about a 'lethal combination of alcohol and painkillers.' Doesn't that beat all? Angela's a bit upset. Seems she liked him 'cause he was nice to her. Call me if you get the chance."

Beep. "Hi, darling. Mom here. Just checking in with you. Dad says hi too. We missed you last Saturday. Your brother was . . ."

Colleen stopped the machine and sat back on the couch. Oh, great. First Roger Cunningham complains about her to Cranford Rhoades, and now Jackson Ramses too. What nerve! She really despised them. And she couldn't believe Bob Jones was dead.

Gillian came from the kitchen carrying two mugs of steaming decaf coffee. The enticing aroma made Colleen's nostrils twitch. She took a mug and sipped carefully. All they needed to make it perfect were some nice French pastries.

"Bob Jones OD'd? What does that do for your case?"

"Nothing really. I don't believe he was involved in Amber's death. It seems awfully lucky for Jackson Ramses though. I think Jones could have caused him some trouble."

Gillian nodded, listening.

Colleen stood up and started pacing the room, thinking aloud. "There's really nothing to indicate that Sheila died any other way than the police said.

152

The heroin was purer than usual and she overdosed. I thought maybe Jackson killed her so he could use Angela instead."

"Colleen, you're a smart girl. You know he'd need more of a motive than that. And there's no way to prove it, is there?"

"No, and I suppose the others could have done it too."

"Others?"

Gillian patted the couch, but Colleen chose to continue pacing. It helped release some of her pent-up energy. "Well, there's Sheila's father for one. He has quite a sadistic streak, but you know that. Plus, he has the money to hire someone to put Sheila out of her misery, so to speak. She was a disappointment and an embarrassment." She paused. "Then there's Randy Wilson. Full of rage and bitterness. He could have done it out of revenge either against Sheila personally or against Starlight. It would embarrass them, put them under scrutiny by the authorities, which her death did indeed do. Or maybe it wasn't even revenge, just a desire to put her at 'peace with the Lord'."

Colleen took a swallow of coffee. She looked at Gillian, who sat on the couch like an attentive student. The sight brought a smile to her lips and an answering one from Gillian.

"Third," Colleen continued, "is Rick Ewing, our weird fan. He's obsessed with her. A stalker really. Leaves her interesting presents. He could have killed her out of jealousy. Some kind of if-I-can't-have-her-no-one-can scenario. Seems harmless to me, though. But if any of those people killed her, it would mean nothing as far the insurance company is concerned. The only one that matters is Jackson, because he's the producer of the video."

"What about some of the other actors? You never know what kinds of petty grievances or jealousies they might have had."

"True."

"And then, there's always Jenna and her group. Some of them can be pretty radical."

Colleen stopped pacing and stared at Gillian askance. She didn't want to think about that possibility.

"Only kidding," Gillian said as she reached up and pulled Colleen into her lap. She kissed Colleen's neck. "Why don't we finish what we started in the elevator?"

"Mmmm," Colleen responded as she guided Gillian's hand to the swell of her breast, "let's pretend we're still in the elevator."

She reached up and turned off the light.

Chapter Fourteen

When Colleen got to the office the next morning, a voice mail told her to report to Cranford Rhoades' office as soon as she got in. So Lisa didn't straighten things out after all. What a way to end the week, Colleen thought as she made a quick cup of coffee. She hadn't had time for any at home because she and Gillian had made love again. It surprised her somewhat, but she decided not to question Gillian's motives and just enjoy it.

She looked in the mirror behind her door. Her tailored blue suit made her ice-blue eyes more vivid and brought out the red-gold highlights in her hair. She smoothed her hair with one hand, glad that she'd finally cut it. Its shoulder length was much more professional-looking than the long unruly curls she'd cursed most of her life. The suit had been expensive, but she had to admit that the cut flattered her full figure. Her white blouse was starched and ironed to perfection, and the cameo at her throat softened the tailored look.

Something must have told her to wear the suit today, she decided as she took one last sip of coffee and headed to the executive wing. She grabbed her notes on the way out. As usual, she marveled at the difference between the rest of the building and the executive suite. She told the secretary that Mr. Rhoades was expecting her. He called Rhoades on the phone and then waved her in.

The head of the firm sat behind his desk and was as immaculately dressed as ever. Not one wrinkle or crease marred the exquisite cut of his charcoal-gray suit. His starched shirt gleamed white, and in the cuffs Colleen swore she saw the glitter of diamonds. His tie was a lighter shade of gray with barely noticeable multicolored speckles. Once again, Colleen was glad that she'd chosen to wear her own new suit that day.

"Please sit down, Miss Fitzgerald." His cultured tone was even.

She sat and waited patiently while he finished looking through some papers before signing them. Buzzing his secretary, he had him come in and retrieve the papers and then turned his attention to Colleen.

"I'm sure Miss Anderson told you that a second

person has filed a formal complaint against this firm, and against you in particular."

"Yes, Mr. Rhoades, I am aware of that."

"I was impressed by the way you handled the Emerson affair, so I'm not inclined to take this as seriously as I might in other circumstances. I am, however, aware that you are still relatively new and perhaps you have been, shall we say, a bit overzealous. Do you have some personal interest in this case?"

"If you mean, do I know the people involved, then no. I do know that I have a slight tendency to get too personal. Lisa has spoken to me about it."

"You took in a minor child?"

"She came to me asking for help. I contacted a lawyer I know, who has since taken the girl into her custody. She's to be reunited with her mother."

He looked at his papers. "I have a copy of your preliminary report here. Seems you think the producer of this video might have murdered the deceased so he could substitute this girl in her place?"

Colleen nervously gripped the edges of her chair. "I don't think I used the term 'murder' in my report, sir."

He looked up and smiled slightly. "So you didn't. Now, have you talked to the police about your suspicions? I know you want to do a good job, but solving crimes is not part of it. I am fully aware of your role in the capture of Albert Simmons in the Candy Emerson case, but you can't be a hero every time."

"I was going to call the police this morning."

"Good. So, *have* you been harassing Mr. Ramses?"

"I've been by to question him several times, but I've maintained a completely professional relationship. Does he feel I've been to see him too often?"

"That seems to be it. I just want you to be careful. Try to question him when he's not working. That way, he can't claim you are costing him money by shutting down production."

Colleen didn't mean to, but she let out an exasperated sigh. "Talking to him after hours could be dangerous. His studio is in Southeast. I can't go there after dark alone."

"Do you need to speak with him again?"

"Maybe just once or twice. Lisa asked me to wrap this up by mid-week. I'm sorry, Mr. Rhoades."

"Colleen, you're doing a good job. We're happy to have you with us. Like I said, I'm not taking Ramses' complaint seriously, but think about what we've talked about."

He closed her file and opened another manila folder. Colleen stood and left the room. In the outer office, the two secretaries appeared to be busy. Colleen glanced at the office Kevin Sampson used to occupy. His name was now off the door. She wondered if a new partner would come in. The sign outside the building and all their business stationery still read "Sampson and Rhoades Investigations."

She hurried back to her office. Reading through her notes, she found the name of the detective who'd investigated Sheila's death and called him. She was lucky; he was in the station rather than on the street. She could tell from his tone that he was annoyed to hear from her.

"I just thought you should know about this new development," she told him. "It gives him a motive to want Sheila Cunningham dead. And don't you think it a little odd that Jackson Ramses' production assistant turns up dead too."

"We see no connection between the two deaths, other than the fact they worked for the same company. I appreciate your concern, Miss Fitzgerald, but the Cunningham case was closed days ago. The fact that Jackson Ramses had another actress to take her place just doesn't seem like motive enough for me. He probably has twenty actresses willing to take her place. These people aren't worth your trouble."

"These people? You don't think Sheila Cunningham is worth your time?"

"Look, the lifestyle they chose makes it pretty certain they'll die a lot sooner than the rest of us. Half of 'em use drugs. They get diseases and spread them. They're scum."

Colleen was angry. "And what about the underage girls who are preyed on by men like Jackson Ramses. Are they scum too?"

"That's a whole different issue. If you know something, I can transfer you to Vice."

"That won't be necessary!"

Colleen slammed the phone down in frustration. All those *Washington Post* articles about the inefficiency of the D.C. police seemed to be more accurate than she'd like to believe. Was there nothing to bring Jackson Ramses down? No matter what she found out about him, it appeared he'd be able to continue doing his sleazy work. He seemed immune to scandal of any kind. Lisa and Cranford Rhoades were right — she needed to step back and be totally impersonal, but whenever she thought of Sheila and Angela, it was hard. Especially after reading some of the Gail Dines book that she'd bought the other night. But it wasn't up to her to be a one-woman crusade against Jackson Ramses.

She called Jenna and asked her to lunch. They had much to talk about, and Colleen didn't feel like doing it on the phone. Jenna agreed to meet her at Food for Thought again.

She spent the morning organizing her notes and decided to type up her final report. Lisa had given her until the middle of next week, but she decided she had nothing new, especially after her talk with Cranford Rhoades. Franklin and Associates would just have to pay the life insurance Starlight had taken out on Amber Rose. *Bad Moon Rising* would go on, but at least Colleen had the satisfaction of knowing Angela would not be part of it.

She caught the subway to DuPont Circle. The cloudless sky allowed the sun to bring a meager warmth to the cold autumn day. When she got to the restaurant, Jenna was already waiting. She stood and smiled as Colleen approached. As usual, Jenna looked immaculate in a black suit and pale burgundy shirt. Colleen could imagine she'd be formidable before a judge.

Jenna kissed Colleen lightly on the mouth and handed her a single iris. "You look stunning, my dear."

"Thank you. It's the first day I've worn this suit." She laughed. "And a good thing too. This morning I got called into Cranford Rhoades' office. He's the surviving partner."

Jenna raised her eyebrow. "Trouble?"

"Not really. Seems ol' Jackson Ramses lodged a complaint against me and my handling of the case.

He says I'm harassing him. Causing production downtime and financial losses."

"Maybe you're getting too close to the truth."

The waitress came over and they ordered lunch. "I've decided to close the case," Colleen said. "I can't find anything to connect him personally or professionally to Sheila's death. My other so-called suspects don't really pan out either. All I'm doing by asking more questions is making people mad."

Jenna sipped her iced tea and looked at Colleen. It made Colleen nervous. "Do I have lipstick on my teeth?" she asked.

"Oh, sorry. I didn't mean to stare. It's just that I find you extremely attractive. I really would like to go out with you. Is that possible?"

"You know I'm seeing Gillian."

"Yes, but do you have a commitment?"

Colleen didn't answer right away. She'd asked herself the same question, but Gillian had been very attentive these last couple of days. They'd made love often. Yet Colleen had to admit she did find Jenna Bolden extremely attractive too. It would be easy to date her while Gillian lived in Rehoboth. But would it be fair to either one? Or to herself, for that matter?

"Jenna, I like you too, but I don't think I'd be comfortable dating two women at the same time."

Jenna's disappointment was obvious, but she quickly joked, "Then I guess you'll have to dump Gillian." She smiled and took Colleen's hand. "I understand. I want to be your friend, and if you need to keep me at arm's length, I accept that."

"Thank you, Jenna. That means a lot to me."

"I don't know how we're going to break the news

to Brian. He's been trying to set us up for a while now."

Colleen laughed. "He is so incorrigible. I think he's more concerned about my love life than I am."

The waitress arrived with their food, and they both ordered a second drink. They ate in silence for a bit before Colleen asked, "How is Angela?"

"Her mother is coming to pick her up tomorrow. It was very generous of Gillian to pay her way. Angela cannot stop talking about her." She laughed. "I think she's developed quite a crush."

Colleen laughed too. "I think you're right."

"I looked into the feasibility of Angela's mother pressing charges against Jackson Ramses and Starlight Studios, but because he's got the requisite signed papers, he's done nothing illegal. Angela had not one, but two fake I.D.'s that 'proved' she was nineteen."

"That man's gonna get off smelling like a rose."

"You think it's just an odd coincidence that Bob Jones died too? I mean, he told Angela someone was trying to kill him."

Colleen pushed her plate away. "I talked to the police earlier. They see no connection and aren't interested in pursuing it further. To them it's just another accidental overdose."

"Yeah, booze and drugs. Never a good combination." Jenna picked up the menu again. "Dessert?"

Colleen debated whether or not to order carrot cake, but remembering Gillian's rock-hard body, she decided against it. She knew it would take more than just turning down one dessert to get into shape herself. And she couldn't help but wonder if Jenna's body was as solid as Gillian's. "Are you a swimmer?" she asked impulsively.

Jenna raised her eyebrow. It was a habit that Colleen was beginning to find endearing. "Yes, I do swim. I also lift weights and run. Why?"

"Oh, you look like a swimmer. Nice broad shoulders." Colleen felt herself blush.

"So, you *have* noticed me?"

Colleen's cheeks felt on fire. Sometimes she was so transparent. How to extricate herself from this situation? "Why don't we pay up and head over to Lambda Rising. I'm sure Brian is working and would love to see us."

Colleen insisted on paying this time. Once outside, she noticed it had gotten a little more nippy. They walked to the bookstore. Unfortunately, Brian was off for the afternoon. Colleen felt bad; it had been over a week since she'd seen him. She resolved to call him at home that night. Jenna called a cab and had the driver take Colleen back to her office first. They sat together in the backseat, the sexual tension between them palpable. Colleen didn't know what to say. She resisted the urge to take Jenna's hand. The cool air outside had done little to diminish the heat in her face. She patted her cheeks nervously. A quick glance at Jenna revealed her smiling rather secretively.

When the cab pulled up outside her office, Colleen quickly thanked Jenna and hurried into the building. In the office, she reread her report on the Cunningham case, but couldn't bring herself to E-mail it to Lisa just yet. She pulled out the preliminary information on the ferret case, laughing out loud as she read the particulars. A ferret named Beauregard stood to receive almost half a million dollars, that is, if the dead man's relatives didn't get their hands on it first.

Finally, it was time to leave. She hurried home, sure that Gillian had some excellent plan to start the weekend.

After lunch, Jenna had trouble concentrating at work. It was getting harder and harder to spend time with Colleen. She constantly thought about kissing her. Just that morning in a meeting she had stumbled over her words as an image of Colleen came unbidden to her mind. That glorious red hair and those blue eyes were enough to drive any woman crazy.

When Gillian returned to Rehoboth — and Jenna had no doubt that she would — Jenna decided she'd pull out all the stops and pursue Colleen. It wasn't right that Colleen should be left alone all those nights. There was passion in that body to be released, and Jenna believed she was just the woman to do it.

When her last client canceled at the last minute, she decided to call it a day. Maybe a few laps in the pool would release some of her own frustration. After giving her secretary the rest of the afternoon off too, she drove quickly to her Georgetown condo to grab her workout clothes and then headed to the gym.

She belonged to an exclusive and expensive gym run by two gay men. It boasted state-of-the-art exercise equipment and an Olympic-sized pool where Jenna liked to spend most of her time. She had a personal trainer for when she lifted weights, but

Friday was not her usual day, so she didn't have an appointment. She decided to do it on her own, and started with a warm-up on the stationary bike, something she found extremely tedious but necessary. It was also a time for contemplation, and Jenna found herself thinking of Colleen yet again.

It was impossible to think of the pretty redhead without eventually thinking of Gillian too. Jenna knew the circumstances of Colleen and Gillian's meeting, and she had done her own research into what turned out to be the murder of bodybuilder Candy Emerson. She'd also done some checking into Gillian Smith. She'd found out about the forgery conviction for which Gillian had received probation. Gillian had gone to N.Y.U. and then done the competitive aerobics circuit. The thought of it made Jenna pedal faster. To look at Gillian, it didn't seem like she had given up competing. Jenna felt an adrenaline rush that she could only attribute to a feeling of rivalry. How would Colleen compare Gillian's body to Jenna's?

Twenty minutes later, she slowed down and wiped the sweat from her face. As she stepped off the bike, she did a double take. Was that really Gillian walking into the room? Jenna couldn't help but admire the muscled body shown off so well in tight shorts and a sleeveless T-shirt. Her deep summer tan had yet to fade. She exuded confidence.

Jenna approached. "Hey, Gillian. Want to work out together?"

If Gillian was surprised to see her, she didn't show it. "Jenna."

"Are you a member here?"

"No. My friend Stephan knows the owners. He

arranged for me to work out here when I'm in town."

"You don't come here very often then, do you?" Jenna smiled when she saw the barb hit home.

"That will be changing soon, I assure you."

Jenna lifted two fifteen-pound dumbbells and started doing curls. "Colleen getting a little tired of spending her nights alone? I'm sure there's any number of women who would love to keep her company."

"And you're right there at the head of the line, aren't you, counselor? Well, don't worry, I can take of Colleen just fine on my own." She turned her back on Jenna and then turned around again. "And thanks, but I don't work out with amateurs."

Jenna watched her walk away. Despite Gillian's insult, Jenna couldn't help but notice that she had the tightest ass Jenna had ever seen. Her muscles rippled with every step she took, reminding Jenna of a hunting lioness. Jenna threw down the dumbbells. Maybe she'd swim after all.

Chapter Fifteen

Monday morning, Colleen reread her final report. It was quite a letdown after the excitement of her last case, but that was no reason to drag this out. Maybe she should talk to everyone one more time? It couldn't hurt. The challenge would be tracking them all down. She called Roger Cunningham first. The man on the other end — she assumed he was the snotty butler — told her Mr. Cunningham would not return until that evening. He grudgingly made an appointment for her to come by at seven. She'd hit the end of rush hour on the beltway, but it couldn't be helped. Next, Jackson Ramses agreed to see her at noon. He did not sound happy, but when she explained this would probably be her last interview with him, he rang off in a more cheerful mood.

Randy Wilson and Rick Ewing were the difficult ones. Neither had a fixed address, and her calls to low-rent motels and shelters turned up empty. On impulse, she called Jackson Ramses back. No, he didn't know where either man was staying in D.C., but that fool Randy was in the parking lot again raving as usual. She didn't ask, but he also volunteered that Rick Ewing was there too. Colleen thanked him and hung up.

She looked at her watch. It was almost ten. Her appointment with Jackson was at noon. She surely could spend two hours with Randy and Rick. She then called Jenna's office. She really should talk to her once more to ask additional questions about the members of her anti-porn group. She'd spoken by phone with the ones who'd protested the day Amber died, but you never knew when there might be a zealot or two. The secretary said Ms. Bolden was free at four. Colleen placed her report in the Starlight file. She wouldn't send it to Lisa just yet.

She decided to take a cab to the studio. She'd take her chances finding one to bring her back to the office. When they heard the Southeast address, the first three cabs refused to take her there. It was against the law, but she didn't have the energy to take down their license numbers and pursue it. The fourth cabbie agreed not only to take her to the warehouse, but to come back and pick her up. He gave her his cell phone number.

The now-familiar red brick warehouse came into

view. She got out of the cab and headed toward Sheila's trailer. Sure enough, Rick Ewing was placing fresh flowers all along the steps. He must spend his whole disability check on them, she thought. This time he included photos of the dead woman among the bouquets. They all showed a seductive blonde in various stages of undress. Colleen was sure they came off the video boxes of Amber Rose's movies.

A moving van sat parked near the building and to the right. Colleen figured that the video shoots were finally ending and Starlight Studios, Inc., would be vacating the premises. To her liking, it couldn't be too soon.

To the left of the moving van and between two other trailers, Colleen could see Randy Wilson. He was gesticulating and waving a Bible high above his head. He had a pretty good-sized crowd, and judging by the number of cameras, some of the people were either tourists or reporters. This warehouse had become quite notorious, both for the kind of movies being filmed there and for Amber Rose's death. Every once in a while, two or three people would clap and cheer at something Randy said. Standing near the group, but not part of it, were a few women Colleen recognized from Jenna's anti-porn group. It didn't look as if Randy's followers would be going anywhere soon, so Colleen decided to talk first to Rick.

"Hi there, Mr. Ewing," she called out as she approached Amber's trailer.

He looked up from rearranging the photos. "Miss Fitzgerald, is it? I remember visiting your office." He waved at the display. "Wasn't she beautiful?"

"Yes," she answered truthfully. "Mr. Ewing, I just want to ask you some final questions." She flipped open her notebook. "You said you were at the pharmacy when Amber died. Did you see her in her trailer before you left?"

"No. I watched the filming for a bit. That stupid Ramses fellow didn't know I'd found a way in. There was a little window I could watch from. Poor Amber was having a hard time that day. Jackson was yelling at her a lot. She looked tired. I had to leave when they started the blow-job scene again." He licked his lips. His hands strayed to his crotch.

Colleen averted her eyes, staring instead at a gorgeous pink rose. "And when you got back, Amber was already dead?"

"Yes."

"Have you ever talked to Hobie, the drug supplier?"

He was indignant. "I don't do that sort of thing."

"I don't think you do," Colleen soothed. "I just thought that because you were so concerned about Amber, you might have tried to stop him from bringing the heroin."

Ewing went back to arranging and rearranging the flowers and photos. "He's a funny fella, that one. As much as I hung out here, I never did see him."

"How did you feel when you saw Amber with other men? Protective? Maybe a little jealous? Angry?"

"Sometimes it pissed me off, but I was never mad at her. Amber could be so nice. She smiled at me and even invited me in once."

"Did she ever tell you she was afraid of Jackson Ramses, or anyone else for that matter?"

He shook his head. "Funny thing. She talked to

me about her daddy. Said he was going to come rescue her. Guess he was too late."

"Guess so," Colleen answered, feeling something akin to pity for the man before her. He would probably spend the rest of his life building shrines to a woman who most likely despised him and men like him. "Thanks for your time." He waved distractedly. Colleen moved toward the people clustered around Randy Wilson. She spoke to a woman from Jenna's group. "What's going on?"

"Same thing that's been happening every day since Starlight got here. Randy Wilson, ex porn star, haranguing about sin and hell and damnation. Trying to save our souls." She laughed without humor. "Strange thing is, we're here for the same reason. We want to save these women too, but in a different way."

"Were you here the day Amber Rose died?"

"No. If I recall correctly, it was raining that day. I'm not that dedicated. I know Jenna was here for a bit with a few others. I was shocked to hear the news."

Colleen smiled her thanks and moved away. She consulted her notes. Randy was here that day. He could have waited for Amber in her trailer and . . . And what? Forced her to take the heroin? That wouldn't have been necessary. Maybe he substituted the purer stuff? He would know how to get it. Who to see. But that was assuming he used drugs too. It was hard to believe someone born-again would commit murder, but she also knew that some fanatics used religion to justify all kinds of crimes.

Still, Colleen's gut feeling ruled out Randy Wilson.

Maybe it was the prejudice on her part wanting Jackson Ramses to be the culprit. She decided she didn't need to talk to Randy at that moment. And she certainly would rule out Jenna. No, her money was on the man who waited for her inside.

The heavy door to the warehouse resisted her first efforts to open it. She finally pushed it open, breaking a fingernail in the process. Cursing under her breath, she crept through the dimly lit corridor once again to the set, careful to make no noise. She was early for her appointment. She peeked into the big, bright room. The dark-haired actress known as Tiffany Glass was doing a slow striptease for the actor Chris Iverson. His hand was inside his boxer shorts. Colleen turned away and sat on the floor near the door, glad she'd worn pants that day. She could hear the murmur of voices. When they stopped, she'd go in. If Jackson kept his appointment, she had twenty minutes to wait.

She was beginning to get a chill from sitting on the cement floor, when she became aware that the voices had stopped. She stood and stretched her cramped muscles and then looked in the big room again. It was empty. Her shoes sounded loud against the floor as she made her way to Jackson's office. She knocked once and went in.

Jackson Ramses sat behind his desk, looking at publicity photos of the actors. Colleen was startled again by his handsome good looks.

"Want to help me pick out a picture for the video cover?" he asked without looking at her.

"No, thank you. I'd rather talk about Amber."

He looked at her then and folded his hands across the photos strewn across the desk. "I hope you weren't upset that I went to your boss. I just couldn't have you popping in here anytime you damn well felt like it."

"You could have called and told me that personally."

"I suppose." He smiled. "You know, you're quite good-looking. I could make you a star."

Colleen hoped her contempt showed in her face. "That line may work on sixteen-year-old runaways, but not me, Mr. Ramses." The smug smile left his face as she continued, "By the way, Angela White's mother will be here soon to take her home."

He scowled. "There's more where she came from. Now, what do you want?"

He's not so handsome now, Colleen thought as she said, "Tell me once again where you were when Amber died."

"I was here. In the building. The others verified that for you, if I'm not mistaken."

"Did you buy high-grade heroin from Hobie and substitute it for what Amber normally used?"

If he was taken aback by her blunt question, he did not show it. "I told you I didn't know she was using drugs."

Colleen rolled her eyes. "C'mon, Jackson, we both know you're lying. What kind of security do you have around here anyway?"

"We have a night watchman to protect the equipment in the warehouse. The actors are responsible for keeping their trailers locked when they're not in them."

She wanted to slap the smirk off his face. "Why don't you just come clean with me? You killed Amber for the insurance money because you wanted to use

Angela in her place. Amber wasn't performing. She was causing production overruns. I can see why you'd want to get rid of her."

"For the last time, I did not kill Amber. We may have had problems, but she was my best girl. Listen, with street drugs, you never know what you're gonna get. Whoever packaged up the heroin Amber got that day didn't do his job. That's all. The police cleared me of all suspicion."

"What do you make of Bob Jones turning up dead too? Was he insured?"

"No, we don't insure assistants and the like. It's more important for the actors, in case one of them quits or gets hurt. Or dies. Bob didn't like my style. We had it out. He left. End of story."

Colleen marveled at Jackson's seeming lack of concern. Did nothing move him? "He thought someone was trying to kill him."

Jackson shuffled through the photos again. "Bob Jones was a depressed paranoid schizophrenic. Those prescription drugs he OD'd on — Haldol and Nardil — made a potent combination with the cheap red wine he liked to drink. Poor S.O.B. The doctors said he had a hypertensive crisis. I was sorry to hear about it."

"Did you ever meet Amber's father?"

He held a photo up to the light and nodded his head. Colleen wasn't sure the nod was in answer to her question or in agreement with his choice of photo. He turned the photo to face her and smiled. "Perfect, wouldn't you say?"

The photo showed all five actors — Chris, Tiffany, Julia, Douglas, and Amber — on the bed, seemingly roped together in some sort of perverse sex chain. The sight made Colleen's stomach turn. She turned away.

"It's a shame Amber went and killed herself. I don't think I can use this picture."

"I really don't care to discuss this," Colleen said contemptuously. "I find it, and you, revolting."

He smiled. Again, she had the urge to slap his handsome face. "I'm just exercising my basic First Amendment rights. Just ask that lawyer friend of yours. Jenna something or other. That group she belongs to tried to shut me down, but she had to tell them to back off. Ironic, isn't it?" He closed the folder on the photos. "Now, if you have no further questions, I think this interview is over."

Colleen stood. She really did despise him. "I'll see myself out." She made sure to slam the door behind her. Her heels clacked angrily against the floor. She barely glanced at the king-size bed as she walked through the warehouse one last time and down the corridor to the outside. The cold air felt brittle, but she breathed deeply, as if to cleanse her system. She felt her eyes grow wet, and she angrily wiped the tears away. It wasn't her job to save the Julias and Tiffanys of the world.

Colleen pulled the cell phone from her purse and called the cab driver. He said he'd be there in 20 minutes. She headed over to where Randy Wilson was still speaking. He seemed much more calm than before. Only four people remained listening to him. One had a tape recorder.

"Amber paid for her sins," Randy intoned. " 'Come out of her, my people, lest you share in her sins, and

lest you receive her plagues.' I pray for all of you."
He bowed his head and caressed his Bible, his lips
moving silently.

"The guy's a real nut case," the woman on
Colleen's left whispered to her.

"He's just passionate," Colleen answered, suddenly
irritated.

The woman moved away and said something to
her male companion. They both looked at Colleen as
if she'd sprouted a second head. She was about to
make a face at them when they moved away and got
into a green Cadillac Seville. She noticed the New
Jersey plates as they drove away. "Damn tourists,"
she muttered under her breath.

Colleen approached Randy and touched his arm
gently. He stopped his silent prayer and looked at
her. He didn't seem to recognize her. "May I help
you, my sister?"

"I'd just like to talk to you about Amber Rose's
death."

"I pray that she took Jesus into her heart in her
final moments."

"Where you with her in those moments? Did you
kill her?"

Randy held up a hand in protest. "I did not. That
would be a sin, to take the life of another. But for
the will of God, I would be dead too. He has given
me a mission despite this scourge He has laid upon
me."

Thinking of Phillip, Colleen could only feel
compassion for Randy. She knew the horror that was
AIDS. If his belief in God helped Randy deal with it,
then who was she to begrudge him that?

"Starlight will be leaving soon," she said.

His eyes blazed with feverish brightness. "Then I will follow them, for they must know what they have done. And I will teach the others. 'The body is not for sexual immorality but for the Lord.' Corinthians, one-six-twelve."

Colleen smiled. She couldn't think of anyone else she'd rather have hounding Jackson Ramses and his disgusting video company — she glanced over at Amber's trailer — except perhaps Rick Ewing. Her taxi pulled up, and as she turned away, Randy pressed a tiny booklet into her hand. In the back of the cab, she looked at the Bible tract. "The Evils of Homosexuality" it read. With a shake of her head, she stuffed it between the seats.

Chapter Sixteen

Back at the office, Colleen resolutely typed up what would truly be her final report. She left spaces for her last interviews with Jenna Bolden and Roger Cunningham. She strolled over to Lisa Anderson's office and poked her head inside.

"Hey, Lisa. Just want to let you know I'll have the final report on the Cunningham case on your desk first thing in the morning."

"Great, a day early. We can talk about the ferret case." Lisa grinned.

"Oh, goodie."

"What's on for the rest of the day?"

Colleen came into the office and sat down. "I've got two more people to interview and then I'm done. One appointment is at four, the other at seven."

"This was a hard assignment for you, wasn't it?"

"Yes. The whole pornography thing . . . Well, it just disturbed me. But at least I got a young girl out of the clutches of that jerk."

Lisa smiled. "Mr. Rhoades has already received a thank-you call from the mother about that. I wouldn't be surprised if you got a little bonus because of it."

"Thanks." Colleen stood. She couldn't wait to tell Gillian. Just the thought of her made Colleen step more briskly down the hall. The answering machine clicked on when she called home, and she decided not to leave a message. She grabbed her purse and took a cab to Jenna's office.

Colleen was impressed with the prestigious Georgetown address of Jenna's law firm. Her name wasn't yet on the door, and Colleen wondered if she was on the track to partner. She was momentarily awestruck as she entered the receptionist's area. It was three times the size of her own firm's executive wing. The imported gold-veined black marble floor reflected both sunlight and the people who walked across it, and the walls were covered with rich fabric wallpaper in hues of gold and burgundy. The sun streaming through oversized windows caressed exotic tropical plants, most of which Colleen couldn't even name.

The receptionist sat a desk twice the size of Mr. Rhoades'. The striking brunette looked like she had just stepped out of the pages of *Vogue*. Colleen was sure the woman's ivory wool suit cost more than Colleen's weekly salary. A gold nameplate identified her as Heather Anderson. She looked up and smiled as Colleen approached. "May I help you?"

Colleen self-consciously smoothed her own plain, gray wool slacks. "I have an appointment with Jenna Bolden."

Heather looked through a gilt-edged appointment book. "Ms. Fitzgerald?"

"Yes."

"I'll buzz you through."

The double glass doors to the left didn't buzz, they chimed. Colleen smiled and walked through. On the other side, another receptionist, this one a strawberry blonde and as expensively dressed as Heather, waited to meet her. Colleen felt funny following her down the carpeted hallway. This unnamed femme fatale walked a model's walk, swaying her hips like she was on a designer's runway. Her blue silk suit glided and undulated, more like a sexy nightgown than business attire, over her superb body. Colleen wondered if Cindy Crawford beauty was a prerequisite for working there. The woman stopped before a door with Jenna's name emblazoned on it, in gold, of course, and motioned for Colleen to enter.

Inside, yet another receptionist — or, most likely, Jenna's secretary — was seated in a small outer office. She wasn't quite as stunning as the two before. In fact, she had a slight butch air about her. The two exchanged a look that convinced Colleen that she was family, but before either could say anything, Jenna poked her head out of her office and motioned for Colleen to come in.

The room was as opulent as the anterooms. What

was it that Jenna said she practiced? Family law? Colleen would never have imagined it would pay this well. She sat in one of the Ethan Allen chairs that faced Jenna's polished redwood desk.

"This is quite an office," was all Colleen could say.

"You're offended?"

"Well ... I wouldn't say that exactly."

"I've worked hard to get where I am, and I think I've managed to maintain my integrity. I don't defend drug dealers or murderers, and I truly believe in my clients." Her tone was slightly defensive.

"You'll have to explain to me sometime how 'family law' translates into something so obviously profitable."

Jenna smiled, obviously relieved. "It's a date. Now, what can I do for you today? Are you here about Angela?"

"I'm just wrapping up my notes on the Amber Rose case. I wanted to interview everyone one more time. You and your group were protesting at the studio the day Amber died. You're positive no one left the group, disappeared for even a little while? To go to the bathroom perhaps?"

"I told you before that we had all left before she died."

"Someone could have gone to Amber's trailer and substituted pure heroin for what she usually used. Maybe someone from your group who wasn't with you that morning, but came later on their own?"

Jenna frowned. "I can pretty much guarantee that no one in my group uses drugs, let alone knows how to obtain them. They wouldn't know the difference between pure heroin and sugar."

"But you would."

The words were out before Colleen could stop them. Jenna did not answer right away. Her dark eyes blazed with anger. Her broad shoulders visibly stiffened.

"I think you know me well enough by now to know that I would *never* do such a thing."

"I . . . I'm truly sorry. It's just that this case is driving me nuts. I'm sure Jackson Ramses is the guilty one, but I have absolutely no proof. I'm frustrated."

Jenna's shoulders relaxed. Her voice softened. "I know it's hard. Amber lived a brutal life and died an even more brutal death. She had everything. Wealth. Education. Beauty. Intelligence. You wonder how someone like that could fall so low, but we're all human. Even the privileged have insecurities." She laughed mirthlessly. "Listen to me. I sound like some talk show host."

Colleen stood. "I'm sorry to have taken up your time. Like I said, I just wanted to talk to everyone involved one more time. I'll be seeing Mr. Cunningham tonight, and then I'm finished. Amber becomes another statistic and Starlight Studios becomes fifty grand richer."

Jenna stood too. "Hey, at least you helped save Angela White. She's on her way home, thanks to you. No statistic, that one."

Colleen smiled. "Thank you for that. I'll be seeing you."

"Colleen, wait!" Jenna quickly came around the desk and grabbed her. They stood so close together that Colleen could feel the heat from Jenna's body. Her strong fingers seemed to burn through Colleen's jacket. Colleen felt that rush of feeling that made her scalp tingle and her breath come in gasps. Her knees felt weak. Jenna's dark eyes smoldered with unspoken passion as she leaned down and kissed Colleen full on the lips, her tongue soft at first and then more demanding. Colleen's hands seemed to rise on their own to grasp Jenna's head, her fingers gliding through Jenna's wonderful thick hair. She heard herself moan against Jenna's insistent mouth, and then Jenna's hands were stripping her of her jacket. Jenna slid Colleen's white cotton blouse up from her waistband. It was the shock of Jenna's cool fingers against Colleen's burning skin that almost broke the spell.

Colleen tried to push away, but Jenna held fast as she kissed Colleen's neck. Somehow, Colleen's blouse was open as Jenna's mouth continued its journey, leaving burning prints down Colleen's throat and across her shoulders. When Jenna reached the mounds of flesh bursting from Colleen's bra, Colleen couldn't help but pull Jenna's head closer. Her moans were loud even to her own ears, but she couldn't seem to stop herself.

The shrill ring of the phone startled them both. Colleen sagged back into her chair as Jenna reach for the offensive instrument. Jenna was as flushed as Colleen felt. Colleen rebuttoned her blouse with shaking fingers.

Jenna's voice sounded irritated. "What? Now? You can't stall him? Oh, okay. Give me five minutes." She hung up the phone and turned to Colleen. "I'm so sorry. It's the senior partner of the firm. He's on his way here now."

Colleen managed to shrug into her suit jacket.

She patted her hot cheeks. "I don't know what came over me. That shouldn't have happened."

Jenna grinned, obviously pleased with herself. "I'm not sorry that it did. You're as passionate as I imagined you would be." She took Colleen's hand and kissed it gently. "I'd like to see you again."

Colleen snatched her hand away. Her skin tingled where Jenna's lips had touched. "We've already talked about this. We can't see each other again. At least, not like you mean. I've got a girlfriend."

"Gillian Smith? I don't think I'm wrong when I say she hasn't made a commitment to you."

"You don't know our situation."

Jenna smiled again. Colleen had to look away. She wasn't sure she could resist the temptation of those dark eyes.

"You call me when you're ready. Next time Gillian leaves you to return to the salt, sand, and sea gulls."

Colleen draped her purse over her shoulder and tried to ignore what Jenna said, but some part of her didn't want to. She couldn't deny the feelings Jenna aroused in her. But what was she going to do about it? For now, she just smiled briefly and walked out the door. She couldn't resist a backward glance. Jenna was sitting behind her desk once more, seemingly fully composed. She nodded to Colleen, flashing a cocky smile that made Colleen's heart beat faster. Colleen walked out quickly, almost running into a tall heavy-set man who entered the inner office. She mumbled her excuses, wondering all the while if Jenna's butchy secretary always looked so smug.

After stopping at a Starbucks to compose herself, Colleen picked up her car and headed out of the city for her appointment with Roger Cunningham. The strong coffee had done little to calm her nerves. She kept reliving the incident in Jenna's office over and over. She could feel the flush spread over her face and her panties grow wet as she remembered Jenna's kisses and mouth against her breasts.

And here she was, making the awful rush-hour drive on Interstate 395, inching her way to the Capital Beltway to make it to McLean by seven. She knew Cunningham's snot-nosed butler would turn her away if she was even one minute late. At least concentrating on the traffic around her made not thinking about Jenna easier.

With five minutes to spare, Colleen pulled into the Cunningham estate. The mansion and the lawn around it blazed with light, allowing her to see the fading but still vibrant colors of the trees and mums. The butler must have heard the crunch of tires on gravel, for the big double doors to the house opened before she was even out of the car.

"Mr. Cunningham is expecting you," he said with disapproval as she approached. He stepped aside. He led her down the long hallway to the library where she'd met Sheila's father before. As Roger turned to greet her, she was struck again by his resemblance to a young Raymond Burr.

"Miss Fitzgerald, I thought this whole ugly affair was settled. Why are you here again?"

"I'm not fully satisfied. This was your daughter who died. Your only child. How can you treat this like some bad investment deal?"

"What do you want from me? I've got plans for that damnable studio. To pay them back for Sheila."

Colleen wasn't about to let him absolve himself of

all blame. "They took advantage of a young woman who was vulnerable, but *you* created that vulnerability. You turned your back on her when she needed you most, and then cruelly taunted her for years with false promises of help."

He was standing directly in front of her, but she wouldn't let him intimidate her. She wouldn't let him see the fear that his hostility created. His voice was barely controlled and chilly. "You know *nothing* of my situation. Sheila broke her mother's heart, turned into a no-good slut. Sheila was welcome anytime she got off the drugs."

Colleen was incensed, the last vestiges of her professional objectivity crumbling. "An addict can't just quit like that." She snapped her fingers. "They need help. You could have provided that help. With your money, you could have sent her somewhere like the Betty Ford Clinic, but you let her die like an animal. And what about her child? Your grandson? Did you ever care about him?"

His tight-lipped silence led her to take Sheila's photo album from her purse. She'd carried it with her ever since she'd found it in the trailer. She flipped to the page of the infant in blue. "Take a good look at your grandson, you heartless bastard!"

He squeezed his eyes shut, like a small child trying to ignore Mommy and Daddy. She half expected him to cover his ears with his hands and start singing "Mary Had a Little Lamb." The silence in the room crackled. Finally, he let out a deep sigh and opened his eyes. With trembling hands, he took the album from her. He sagged against the edge of his massive desk.

"I never saw the child. It was humiliating. My

daughter, giving birth to a bastard. Sheila's mother never forgave me. She cursed me until her dying day and told me she would see me in hell. She blamed herself for not standing up to me, but I was always harsh with them both."

"Did you ever physically abuse them?"

"At times. I'm not proud of it, but my father didn't raise me by sparing the rod."

"You think that excuses you?" Colleen asked.

He looked up from the photo. "Don't you think I've suffered too? My wife dead from cancer. My only child lost to me. A grandson I never knew. I only wanted Sheila's suffering to end. I couldn't bear the thought of her doing those unspeakable things to her body."

Colleen threw up her hands in frustration. "Why did you keep telling her to come home, and then turn her away again and again? She was reaching out to you. Are you that cold inside?"

He didn't answer right away. Instead, he lightly ran his finger over the photo and let a small smile play across his mouth. When he looked at Colleen again, she could swear she saw tears in his eyes, but he tightened his lips once again. "Sheila was a disappointment from the beginning. She did everything she could to hurt me. Like choosing that inferior university in New York when I could have paid for anything — Harvard, Princeton, Yale. She tells me she's a lesbian. Then the drugs, the bastard child. I ask you, what parent could endure that?"

Colleen thought of her own parents and acknowledged the apprehension she felt. Although she hoped not, they could very well react to her lesbianism the same way as Roger Cunningham.

"Which was worse? N.Y.U. or being a lesbian?" she asked cynically.

"Don't toy with me, young lady!"

"Sorry."

"She came to me with this story about being raped and then pregnant," he continued, as if he was dictating his life story. "Just another lie, I thought. Trying to play on her mother's sympathies, but I didn't let Sheila talk to her. That woman, God love her, would have welcomed Sheila back home as if nothing happened. Reward her for all the pain she caused. I couldn't allow it."

"When did you find out that Sheila was doing porno?"

He laughed harshly. "A colleague of mine rented one of her videos. He came to me all smug and superior. Can you believe it? I almost killed him. But that was the last of him."

Colleen was growing afraid again. This man is insane, she thought. "What did you do?"

"Hostile takeover of his company. The idiot ended up committing suicide. He always was weak."

"Is that how you plan to destroy Starlight Studios?"

He laughed as if she'd told some great joke. "Wouldn't that be something? To have my name associated with trash like that. No, my dear. I've planned a little more carefully for that one."

Colleen decided it was time to leave. She held out her hand. "Could I have the album back, please."

He took one last look at the photo of his grandson and handed the album to Colleen. "What? No more questions?"

"I think Jackson Ramses killed your daughter, but I have no proof. Only my own feeling."

Cunningham's laughter rang out yet again. "That stupid man couldn't do anything so important."

Something dawned on her, and she backed away, putting the heavy leather chair between them. "You paid him to kill Sheila." It was a statement.

"All he had to do was get the right drugs. Not that watered-down crap she normally used. He never came through. If you want something done right, you have to do it yourself." His eyes took on a faraway look. "Hobie never even knew who I was. No one did. I liked the anti-porn group." He looked right at Colleen. "They allow men, you know."

Colleen remembered fleetingly that she'd never shown Jenna the picture of Roger Cunningham. Damned idiot! she chided herself. She glanced at the closed door and wondered how fast she could get out. Roger's voice droned on. "That last day I dressed like a homeless man. Hung around the warehouse, sipping that god-awful cheap wine they drink. When that Jesus freak started going off and had everyone's attention, I just snuck into Sheila's trailer and left my little present."

"She never saw you?" Colleen couldn't help asking.

Sadness finally crept into his face. "She was so wasted. My beautiful Sheila. She wouldn't have known if King Kong was in there. I watched her. It happened very quickly. I paid top dollar for the purest stuff Hobie could find."

He went around the desk. Colleen watched him warily and edged toward the door. In seemingly slow motion, he took a handgun from the drawer and pointed it at her. A calm seemed to descend over his features and he smiled, the glitter of insanity brightening his eyes. Blue eyes, just like Sheila's, Colleen thought incongruously as she opened her mouth to scream.

Chapter Seventeen

In her nightmare, Colleen revisited the Cunningham estate. Her conversation with Roger played out again and again like an endless tape. He took the gun from his desk drawer, but this time it was her lifeless body that fell to the floor while he laughed and laughed. Sheila rose through the floor and beckoned her, the skin rotting off her body. With a scream, Colleen woke terrified, her eyes frantically searching the blackness. At the bottom of the bed, Smokey jumped up in alarm, his cat eyes glittering in the dark. Strong arms pulled her close.

"Colleen, Colleen. It's okay!"

She woke fully and asked guiltily, "Did I wake you?"

"You were having a bad dream again. Do you feel okay?" Her hand softly touched Colleen's forehead. "I think you have a fever."

Colleen flung the covers off; they were soaked on her side of the bed. She snuggled deeper into Gillian's arms. "It's just too warm in here. What time is it, anyway?"

Gillian glanced at the clock. "It's almost six. At least you slept through the night this time." She kissed Colleen on the neck. "We could go back to sleep," she said, "or we could do something else . . ."

Colleen stiffened. She hadn't been able to make love with Gillian all week. "On second thought," Gillian soothed, "you just go back to sleep." She patted the bed for Smokey to come up. "Here. Snuggle with your feline."

She worried that fear of the nightmare would prevent her from falling asleep, but as she curled around both her cat and Gillian, she felt her body finally relax.

When she awoke again, Colleen stretched, kicking the cat off the bed. She felt around for Gillian and was disappointed to find her gone. The clock said it was nearly nine. She could smell the aroma of freshly brewed coffee and — she sniffed — cinnamon rolls? She kicked the covers off as she remembered that today was the day Phillip and Stephan would arrive from Rehoboth to celebrate Halloween in the city.

By the time Colleen had brushed her teeth, Gillian had folded up the bed and opened the curtains to let in the bright sunshine. On the way to the kitchen, she stopped to sniff the gorgeous bouquet of white roses Jenna had sent as a get-well token. She smiled as she glimpsed Gillian's jealous little frown.

On Colleen's little breakfast table Gillian had laid out a coffee mug and a plate of cinnamon buns. Colleen kissed her full on the mouth. Gillian's arms tightened around her. "You are so wonderful," Colleen murmured. "I'll take cinnamon buns over roses any day. I didn't know you could bake."

Gillian laughed. "Yes, me and the Pillsbury Doughboy. Feel better now?"

Colleen took a sip of coffee. It was good and strong. "I still can't believe what happened. I was so sure Jackson Ramses was responsible for Sheila's death, and it turned out to be her own father."

"He was a cold, heartless man. I think he and my father were cut from the same cloth." Her expression grew sad. "Sheila and I were a lot alike too. We're both only children who disappointed their wealthy fathers and rebelled. I wonder sometimes what might have happened if we'd stayed together in college. I wouldn't have let her deteriorate like that."

"That was long time ago, darling. You certainly can't blame yourself."

"I wonder what made him do it?"

"What? Kill himself or his daughter or both?" Colleen bit into a cinnamon roll. It was warm and delicious.

"He could have gotten away with murder, you know. What made him confess to you?"

"I don't know. It was after I told him I thought Jackson Ramses was responsible. He seemed insulted that I thought Jackson had the brains to pull it off.

193

When he pointed that gun at me . . ." Colleen shivered at the memory. Though nearly a week had passed, it seemed like yesterday.

Taking Colleen's hand, Gillian said, "Thank God he turned the gun on himself."

"Let's talk about something else. Have you heard from Phillip and Stephan?"

"Stephan called last night to say they should arrive by noon." She looked at her watch. "Which gives you exactly one hour to get dressed. The limo's taking them directly to the hotel."

Colleen jumped up and headed to the shower, deciding against enticing Gillian to join her. During the past week, she'd resisted Gillian's advances. She recalled that she'd done the same after the trauma in Rehoboth Beach. The memory of being trussed up in Albert Simmons' deserted gym, waiting for him to return and kill her, kept creeping into her consciousness. It took weeks before she could relax again.

This time, the shock of seeing someone kill himself right in front of her was almost too much to bear. She tried not to think about it, but the vision came unbidden at all hours of the night and day. Even in the shower, with the warm water gently caressing her, she saw Roger Cunningham move the gun from her to his mouth and pull the trigger. She'd screamed at exactly the same moment, the sight of exploding blood and brain tissue searing into her memory as she fell to the floor in a dead faint.

She'd regained consciousness to find a paramedic taking her pulse. Other EMTs worked futilely on Cunningham. The butler stood in the doorway, his normal stoic countenance replaced with one of utter horror and disbelief. She'd never seen anyone quite so white before, as if all the blood had drained out of his body. At his side stood a smiling Mercy Warner.

She shook the memories from her mind. This would not do. She was safe now, and the whole awful situation was over. Once out of the shower and dressed, she and Gillian headed over to the Ritz-Carlton to find Stephan and Phillip. Their reunion was boisterous. The once frail Phillip hugged Colleen with a strength that surprised her. She was glad she'd helped convince Stephan to bring him home from Mexico. They all settled on the luxurious couches in the sitting area of the suite.

Stephan was looking well. The epitomé of "tall, dark, and handsome," he positively glowed with good health and the happiness of having Phillip with him again.

Phillip was still thin, but she could tell he'd put on weight. His face had lost that gaunt look. His previously buzzcut blonde hair had grown out and was indeed as curly as Colleen had thought it would be. She knew he and Stephan might not be together forever, that unless there was a cure, Phillip would one day succumb to his disease. But at least they would have gotten a few more months — or even years — together.

"So, Gillian tells me you just wrapped up another interesting case," Stephan said.

Colleen squirmed in her seat. "*Interesting* isn't how I'd describe it. Gruesome, maybe." She filled them in on the elements of the case.

"Gotta hand it to you, Colleen," Phillip commented with a chuckle, "you're a natural-born psycho magnet."

"Hey," Gillian said above the laughter, "I hope you're not referring to me!"

"Seriously Colleen, are you sure you want to continue this line of work?" Stephan asked.

Gillian spoke up. "I'd like it if she quit."

"But I like my job," Colleen protested. "I'm sure not all cases will be this exciting or dangerous." She laughed. "As a matter of fact, my next assignment involves a ferret."

Stephan, Phillip, and Gillian all chimed in at once. "A ferret?"

"Yeah, named Beauregard. Beneficiary of almost half a million dollars, and the dead owner's next of kin are not happy. I'll tell you all about it later."

Gillian ordered room service for lunch. Once they were all seated around the table, Colleen said, "I want to hear all about Rehoboth. How are Vera and Suzanne and Bianca? After this weekend, I guess most of the tourists will be gone for the season."

They spent the afternoon catching up on their lives. Then it was time to get ready for the Halloween festivities. The highlight every year was the drag high-heel race down 17th Street. Colleen's friend Brian was participating for the first time. Afterward, brave souls could venture into Georgetown for a costume extravaganza unparalleled anywhere else in the city. It was going to be an exceptional Saturday night. The weather was unseasonably mild, and the darkness would be illuminated by a full harvest moon. It was rare that such a moon fell precisely on Halloween, and most revelers would take full advantage.

Gillian and Colleen returned to the apartment to change into their costumes. Gillian looked dashing as a swashbuckling pirate. Colleen admired the tight fit of her leather pants and knee-high boots. She wore a black vest over a white silk blouse with full sleeves. A real curved sword dangled at her hip, and a jaunty black pirate's hat softened the menacing black patch covering one eye. She even wore a large gold hoop in one ear.

"This thing is going to bug the shit out of me," Gillian said as she adjusted the patch again.

"You look cute without it," Colleen said as she sauntered saucily over to where Gillian stood.

In keeping with their theme, she wore a long, flowing, multi-colored skirt topped with a low-cut white blouse and an elaborately embroidered vest. A new Wonderbra created enticing cleavage. She'd patterned the costume after those worn by the animatronic wenches in Disney's Pirates of the Caribbean theme ride. To finish, she'd threaded black and green velvet ribbons through her curls and strapped a realistic-looking dagger to her waist. When Gillian looked at her, Colleen was rewarded with the pleasure in Gillian's green eyes.

"I'm going to have to fight all the women off of you," Gillian said as she grabbed Colleen and kissed her. She pulled the fabric off Colleen's shoulder and kissed her there too.

"We've got to get back to the hotel," Colleen answered, only half-heartedly pushing her away.

"Okay this time," Gillian growled into her ear, "but tonight you won't turn me away."

"Is that a promise?"

"Let's get out of here before I make us late."

After a quick cab ride to the hotel to pick up Phillip and Stephan, they were back at DuPont

Circle. Phillip wore surgical scrubs, and Stephan wore the simple black leotard and painted white face of a mime. The streets were filled with people dressed in colorful costumes and extravagant drag ensembles of all kinds. It was hard to pick out who wore the most elaborate wig or outrageous makeup. A few people wore street clothes, obviously preferring to remain spectators.

They strolled slowly over to 17th Street, keeping pace with Phillip's slow, sure steps. Gillian started up the stairway to the area's most popular café. Colleen grabbed her arm. "We'll never get a table here tonight."

"Don't worry, I made reservations," she replied as she walked quickly to the hostess stand. When Colleen and the others caught up with her, a vampire maître d' led them to a windowside table. They would have an unobstructed view of the street when the race started because the café had roped off the sidewalk directly in front.

"This place doesn't take reservations," Colleen whispered to Gillian as they opened their menus.

Gillian flashed a grin and a hundred-dollar bill. No other explanation was necessary.

As a clown-clad waiter brought drinks and munchies, Colleen couldn't remember a time when she'd felt happier. She sensed that Gillian would soon be telling her that she planned to move to the city. It wouldn't do for them to move in together right away, Colleen had decided. She liked her cozy studio apartment too much. She would convince Gillian to get an apartment nearby. They could really get to know each other, and Colleen could resolve her feelings for Jenna Bolden. For now, though, she only thought of Gillian and the promises made for later that night.

She looked over at Gillian, smiling at the sight of her in that ridiculous pirate's hat. She'd given up on the eye patch, which suited Colleen just fine. She didn't want anything covering up those wonderful dark green eyes. Stephan and Phillip sat close together, their love for each other never more obvious.

A commotion drew Colleen's attention away from her companions, and suddenly the street was filled with people. Laughing men and a few women ran by, surprisingly steady on absurdly high heels, their colorful costumes flashing and glittering under the street lamps and bright light of the rising moon.

A few of the publications of
THE NAIAD PRESS, INC.
P.O. Box 10543   Tallahassee, Florida 32302
Phone (850) 539-5965
Toll-Free Order Number: 1-800-533-1973
Web Site: WWW.NAIADPRESS.COM
Mail orders welcome. Please include 15% postage.
Write or call for our free catalog which also features an
incredible selection of lesbian videos.

BAD MOON RISING by Barbara Johnson. 208 pp. 2nd Colleen
Fitzgerald mystery.   ISBN 1-56280-211-9 $11.95

RIVER QUAY by Janet McClellan. 208 pp. 3rd Tru North
mystery.   ISBN 1-56280-212-7   11.95

ENDLESS LOVE by Lisa Shapiro. 272 pp. To believe, once
again, that love can be forever.   ISBN 1-56280-213-5   11.95

FALLEN FROM GRACE by Pat Welch. 256 pp. 6th Helen Black
mystery.   ISBN 1-56280-209-7   11.95

THE NAKED EYE by Catherine Ennis. 208 pp. Her lover in the
camera's eye . . .   ISBN 1-56280-210-0   11.95

OVER THE LINE by Tracey Richardson. 176 pp. 2nd Stevie
Houston mystery.   ISBN 1-56280-202-X   11.95

JULIA'S SONG by Ann O'Leary. 208 pp. Strangely
disturbing . . . strangely exciting.   ISBN 1-56280-197-X   11.95

LOVE IN THE BALANCE by Marianne K. Martin. 256 pp.
Weighing the costs of love . . .   ISBN 1-56280-199-6   11.95

PIECE OF MY HEART by Julia Watts. 208 pp. All the
stuff that dreams are made of —   ISBN 1-56280-206-2   11.95

MAKING UP FOR LOST TIME by Karin Kallmaker. 240 pp.
Nobody does it better . . .   ISBN 1-56280-196-1   11.95

GOLD FEVER by Lyn Denison. 224 pp. By author of *Dream
Lover.*   ISBN 1-56280-201-1   11.95

WHEN THE DEAD SPEAK by Therese Szymanski. 224 pp. 2nd
Brett Higgins mystery.   ISBN 1-56280-198-8   11.95

FOURTH DOWN by Kate Calloway. 240 pp. 4th Cassidy James
mystery.   ISBN 1-56280-205-4   11.95

A MOMENT'S INDISCRETION by Peggy J. Herring. 176 pp.
There's a fine line between love and lust . . . ISBN 1-56280-194-5   11.95